THE MAGIC
OF OZ

A FAITHFUL RECORD OF THE REMARKABLE ADVENTURES OF DOROTHY,
TROT, AND THE WIZARD OF OZ, TOGETHER WITH THE COWARDLY LION,
THE HUNGRY TIGER, AND CAP'N BILL, IN THEIR SUCCESSFUL
SEARCH FOR A MAGICAL AND BEAUTIFUL BIRTHDAY
PRESENT FOR PRINCESS OZMA OF OZ

BY

L. FRANK BAUM

"Royal Historian of Oz"

ILLUSTRATED BY

JOHN R. NEILL

For Your Knowledge

The Publisher wishes to express appreciation for the contributions made by
Mr. Robert A. Baum, great-grandson of L. Frank Baum.

This edition was originally published in 1919 by
The Reilly & Britton Company of Chicago, IL

Cover redesign by Steven J. Benedict III
Design and Production team: Mae Barnard, Tina Budzinski,
Lori Holland, and Alison Phillips

Published by For Your Knowledge,
an imprint of Ann Arbor Media Group, LLC
2500 S. State Street, Ann Arbor, MI 48104

Printed and bound in the United States of America
by Edwards Brothers, Inc.

ISBN 1-58726-043-3

06   05   04   03   10 9 8 7 6 5 4 3 2 1

Introduction

nce again, L. Frank answered his correspondents' questions with a very different Oz book. *The Tin Woodman of Oz* took us back in Oz history to answer many of our questions about the Woodman's early life. The quest to find Nick Chopper's girlfriend gave L. Frank a chance to work his magic on the readers. He introduced new characters like Woot the Wanderer, who set the quest in motion, and Captain Fyter, who is almost a double for the Tin Woodman. This character was most likely based on L. Frank's eldest son, Frank J. Baum, who was in the service during World War I. Returning characters included the Wicked Witch of the East, who enchanted Fyter's sword.

In a letter of February 14, 1918, L. Frank indicated to his publisher that he had completed two Oz manuscripts that were to be published following *The Tin Woodman of Oz*. Once again, as he had done with *Rinkitink in Oz,* he was planning ahead, just in case he passed away.

Although he had not talked about it much, my great-grandfather had been in pain for several years and was planning to have his gallbladder removed. The letter went on to say, "But I hope to pull through in good shape. And as the doctors believe this gall trouble has been the cause of my poor health . . . I expect a successful operation will make a new man of me."

In early 1918 he had his gallbladder removed, but recovery was slow, and complicated by an inflamed appendix. L. Frank Baum died on May 6, 1919. He would have been sixty-four on the 15th of May.

If ever there were a title that could encompass all of Oz and what it means to us today, it would be *The Magic of Oz*. This book is full of magic, the magic that has enthralled all who have entered Oz for the last 103 years. As a great-grandson of the Royal Historian, I have had the pleasure of being able to see first hand the effect that this magic has had on people throughout the world.

I have often wondered what might have gone through L. Frank's mind when he held the first copy of *The Wonderful Wizard of Oz?* Did he have any idea of the effect his creation would have more than a hundred years later? The very fact that we still celebrate Oz proves that it transcends time and events. The real success of Oz lies not in the books themselves, but in the family stories and memories people hold dear, especially those of their first encounter with Oz. When I hear these stories, I am convinced that L. Frank was truly a wizard.

My first memory of Oz goes back to when I was seven years old. My parents had taken me to a release of the 1939 MGM movie, "The Wizard of Oz." We sat in the front row, and as the opening credits rolled by on the big screen, I was able to read "From the book by L. Frank Baum." Just at the same moment, my father leaned over and whispered, "That's your great-grandfather!" I had known that for a while, but to see his name so big, and ON A MOVIE SCREEN! Wow! At that moment the magic that is Oz began to enter my life.

During high school, the wife of my English teacher shared with me her passion for Oz. In the early 1920s, as she boarded a train for college, her parents gave her twenty dollars. She knew they had saved the money over a long time and that it was to last for the entire semester. During a layover at one station, she went for a walk around the town. In a store window she saw a set of all fourteen Oz books. She eyed them awhile and considered the money her parents had given her. When the train pulled out of the station, she had fourteen Oz books and only two dollars and fifty cents left for college.

What impressed me most was her willingness to go without other things so that she could be the proud owner of a set of Oz books. She told me that the Oz characters had become her friends and that they gave her a connection to home each time she read the stories. She kept the books in her family, read them to her children, and then to her grandchildren. Oz had become one of her family traditions.

Even on their 1906 trip, L. Frank and Maud saw an example of the magic the Oz books were spreading. While touring one of the ruins near Cairo, Egypt, L. Frank noticed a caravan passing through. Riding on one of the camels was a mother and her daughter. In the girl's hands was a copy of *The Wonderful Wizard of Oz*. He asked the guide to stop them, and he offered to sign the girl's book. After he had signed the book, the girl's mother told him that they had just come across the desert by camel caravan. The girl had been told that she could bring only two things with her. She chose a doll and *The Wonderful Wizard of Oz*.

If you listen carefully for a day or two, you will be surprised how many times you hear some reference made to Oz. It may be "Hi, Munchkin" or "Toto, I don't think we are in Kansas anymore" or "Follow the Yellow Brick Road" or the classic "There is no place like home." Oz has become part of everyday life the world over.

In 1995, my oldest daughter and I went to Mongolia with the American Museum and spent several days hunting for dinosaur fossils in the Gobi. Upon returning to Ulaanbaatar, the capital, we spent several days exploring the city. On a busy street corner I found a sidewalk bookstore. All the books were spread out along a low wall. The owner watched me as I looked through the many books.

Then he came over and asked me in his broken English what I was looking for. *"The Wizard of Oz,"* I replied.

His response surprised me. "Oh, can't keep in shop. I sell all I get real fast. It is best book for little ones." He was smiling from ear to ear. "Real good book!"

The Oz books have weathered many storms over the years. Critics have said that they are too fanciful, have no redeeming qualities, or are not well written. Libraries have banned them. Yet Oz has survived. They are some of the best-selling books of all time and have been translated into some sixty languages. The 1939 MGM movie version of *The Wizard of Oz* has, I believe, been watched by more people than any other movie.

What makes Oz so lasting? Often the most complex questions have the simplest answers. Such is the case with Oz. All of my experiences lead me to one conclusion. L. Frank's success is simply due to his never having lost sight of his audience, the children. He spoke "Child." He did not believe in using long descriptive passages that guided a reader's imagination. His simple descriptions let each reader fill in the pictures, making the reader part of each adventure in Oz.

My great-grandfather was able to entertain children of all ages because he looked at the world through the eyes of a child, just one step beyond reality. Oz is a home away from home, where dreams are real and reality can be put aside. Oz is imagination unleashed, allowing all who enter to soar "somewhere over the rainbow."

I hope you enjoy the magic in *The Magic of Oz* and that it brings you a lot of joy. If you figure out how to pronounce "PYRZQXGL," please let me know!

Ozily yours,

Robert A. Baum

I Dedicate this Book to the
Children of our Soldiers, the
Americans and their Allies,
with unmeasured Pride and
Affection.   L. F. B.

TO MY READERS

Curiously enough, in the events which have taken place in the last few years in our "great outside world," we may find incidents so marvelous and inspiring that I cannot hope to equal them with stories of The Land of Oz.

However, "The Magic of Oz" is really more strange and unusual than anything I have read or heard about on our side of The Great Sandy Desert which shuts us off from The Land of Oz, even during the past exciting years, so I hope it will appeal to your love of novelty.

A long and confining illness has prevented my answering all the good letters sent me — unless stamps were enclosed — but from now on I hope to be able to give prompt attention to each and every letter with which my readers favor me.

Assuring you that my love for you has never faltered and hoping the Oz Books will continue to give you pleasure as long as I am able to write them, I am

Yours affectionately,

L. FRANK BAUM,

" Royal Historian of Oz."

" OZCOT "
at HOLLYWOOD
in CALIFORNIA
1919

LIST OF CHAPTERS

The Magic of Oz

MT.
MUNCH

Mount Munch

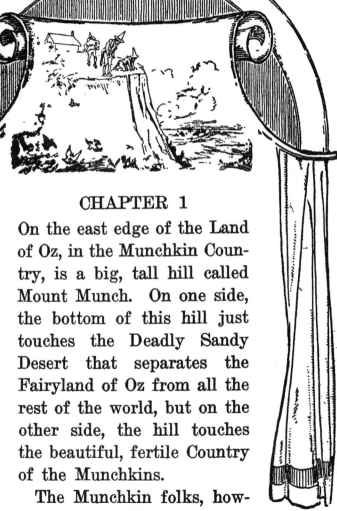

CHAPTER 1

On the east edge of the Land
of Oz, in the Munchkin Country, is a big, tall hill called
Mount Munch. On one side,
the bottom of this hill just
touches the Deadly Sandy
Desert that separates the
Fairyland of Oz from all the
rest of the world, but on the
other side, the hill touches
the beautiful, fertile Country
of the Munchkins.

The Munchkin folks, how-

The Magic of Oz

ever, merely stand off and look at Mount Munch and know very little about it; for, about a third of the way up, its sides become too steep to climb, and if any people live upon the top of that great towering peak that seems to reach nearly to the skies, the Munchkins are not aware of the fact.

But people *do* live there, just the same. The top of Mount Munch is shaped like a saucer, broad and deep, and in the saucer are fields where grains and vegetables grow, and flocks are fed, and brooks flow and trees bear all sorts of things. There are houses scattered here and there, each having its family of Hyups, as the people call themselves. The Hyups seldom go down the mountain, for the same reason that the Munchkins never climb up: the sides are too steep.

In one of the houses lived a wise old Hyup named Bini Aru, who used to be a clever Sorcerer. But Ozma of Oz, who rules everyone in the Land of Oz, had made a decree that no one should practice magic in her dominions except Glinda the Good and the Wizard of Oz, and when Glinda sent this royal command to the Hyups by means of a strong-winged Eagle, old Bini Aru at once stopped performing magical arts. He destroyed many of his magic powders and tools of magic, and afterward honestly obeyed the law. He had never seen Ozma, but he knew she was his Ruler and must be obeyed.

There was only one thing that grieved him. He had discovered a new and secret method of transformations that was unknown to any other Sorcerer. Glinda the Good did not know it, nor did the little Wizard of Oz, nor Dr. Pipt nor old Mombi, nor anyone else who dealt in magic arts. It was Bini Aru's own secret. By its means, it was the simplest thing in the world to transform anyone into beast, bird or fish, or anything else, and back again, once you knew how to pronounce the mystical word: "**Pyrzqxgl.**"

Bini Aru had used this secret many times, but not to cause evil or suffering to others. When he had wandered far from home and was hungry, he would say: "I want to become a cow — **Pyrzqxgl!**" In an instant he would be a cow, and then he would eat grass and satisfy his hunger. All beasts and birds can talk in the Land of Oz, so when the cow was no longer hungry, it would say: "I want to be Bini Aru again: **Pyrzqxgl!**" and the magic word, properly pronounced, would instantly restore him to his proper form.

Now, of course, I would not dare to write down

The Magic of Oz

this magic word so plainly if I thought my readers would pronounce it properly and so be able to transform themselves and others, but it is a fact that no one in all the world except Bini Aru, had ever (up to the time this story begins) been able to pronounce "**Pyrzqxgl**" the right way, so I think it is safe to give it to you. It might be well, however, in reading this story aloud, to be careful not to pronounce **Pyrzqxgl** the proper way, and thus avoid all danger of the secret being able to work mischief.

Bini Aru, having discovered the secret of instant transformation, which required no tools or powders or other chemicals or herbs and always worked perfectly, was reluctant to have such a wonderful discovery entirely unknown or lost to all human knowledge. He decided not to use it again, since Ozma had forbidden him to do so, but he reflected that Ozma was a girl and some time might change her mind and allow her subjects to practice magic, in which case Bini Aru could again transform himself and others at will, — unless, of course, he forgot how to pronounce **Pyrzqxgl** in the meantime.

After giving the matter careful thought, he decided to write the word, and how it should be pronounced, in some secret place, so that he could find it after many years, but where no one else could ever find it.

That was a clever idea, but what bothered the old Sorcerer was to find a secret place. He wandered all over the Saucer at the top of Mount Munch, but found no place in which to write the secret word where others might not be likely to stumble upon it. So finally he decided it must be written somewhere in his own house.

Bini Aru had a wife named Mopsi Aru who was famous for making fine huckleberry pies, and he had a son named Kiki Aru who was not famous at all. He was noted as being cross and disagreeable because he was not happy, and he was not happy because he wanted to go down the mountain and visit the big world below and his father would not let him. No one paid any attention to Kiki Aru, because he didn't amount to anything, anyway.

Once a year there was a festival on Mount Munch which all the Hyups attended. It was held in the center of the saucer-shaped country, and the day was given over to feasting and merry-making. The young folks danced and sang songs; the women spread the tables with good things to eat, and the men played on musical instruments and told fairy tales.

Kiki Aru usually went to these festivals with his

parents, and then sat sullenly outside the circle and would not dance or sing or even talk to the other young people. So the festival did not make him any happier than other days, and this time he told Bini Aru and Mopsi Aru that he would not go. He would rather stay at home and be unhappy all by himself, he said, and so they gladly let him stay.

But after he was left alone Kiki decided to enter his father's private room, where he was forbidden to go, and see if he could find any of the magic tools Bini Aru used to work with when he practiced sorcery. As he went in Kiki stubbed his toe on one of the floor boards. He searched everywhere but found no trace of his father's magic. All had been destroyed.

Much disappointed, he started to go out again when he stubbed his toe on the same floor board. That set him thinking. Examining the board more closely, Kiki found it had been pried up and then nailed down again in such a manner that it was a little higher than the other boards. But why had his father taken up the board? Had he hidden some of his magic tools underneath the floor?

Kiki got a chisel and pried up the board, but found nothing under it. He was just about to replace the board when it slipped from his hand and turned over,

The Magic of Oz

and he saw something written on the underside of it. The light was rather dim, so he took the board to the window and examined it, and found that the writing described exactly how to pronounce the magic word **Pyrzqxgl**, which would transform anyone into anything instantly, and back again when the word was repeated.

Now, at first, Kiki Aru didn't realize what a wonderful secret he had discovered; but he thought it might be of use to him and so he took a piece of paper and made on it an exact copy of the instructions for pronouncing **Pyrzqxgl**. Then he folded the paper and put it in his pocket, and replaced the board in the floor so that no one would suspect it had been removed.

After this Kiki went into the garden and sitting beneath a tree made a careful study of the paper. He had always wanted to get away from Mount Munch and visit the big world — especially the Land of Oz — and the idea now came to him that if he could transform himself into a bird, he could fly to any place he wished to go and fly back again whenever he cared to. It was necessary, however, to learn by heart the way to pronounce the magic word, because a bird would have no way to carry a paper with it, and Kiki would be unable to resume his proper shape if he forgot the word or its pronunciation.

So he studied it a long time, repeating it a hundred times in his mind until he was sure he would not forget it. But to make safety doubly sure he placed the paper in a tin box in a neglected part of the garden and covered the box with small stones.

By this time it was getting late in the day and Kiki wished to attempt his first transformation before his parents returned from the festival. So he stood on the front porch of his home and said:

"I want to become a big, strong bird, like a hawk —**Pyrzqxgl!**" He pronounced it the right way, so in a flash he felt that he was completely changed in form. He flapped his wings, hopped to the porch railing and said: "Caw-oo! Caw-oo!"

Then he laughed and said half aloud: "I suppose that's the funny sound this sort of a bird makes. But now let me try my wings and see if I'm strong enough to fly across the desert."

For he had decided to make his first trip to the country outside the Land of Oz. He had stolen this secret of transformation and he knew he had disobeyed the law of Oz by working magic. Perhaps Glinda or the Wizard of Oz would discover him and punish him, so it would be good policy to keep away from Oz altogether.

Slowly Kiki rose into the air, and resting on his broad wings, floated in graceful circles above the saucer-shaped mountain-top. From his height, he could see, far across the burning sands of the Deadly Desert, another country that might be pleasant to explore, so he headed that way, and with strong, steady strokes of his wings, began the long flight.

The Hawk

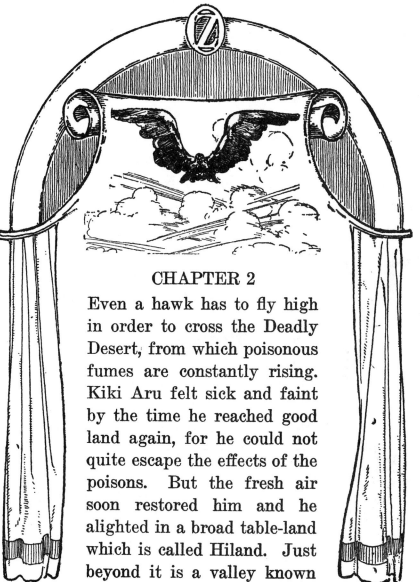

CHAPTER 2

Even a hawk has to fly high in order to cross the Deadly Desert, from which poisonous fumes are constantly rising. Kiki Aru felt sick and faint by the time he reached good land again, for he could not quite escape the effects of the poisons. But the fresh air soon restored him and he alighted in a broad table-land which is called Hiland. Just beyond it is a valley known

The Magic of Oz

as Loland, and these two countries are ruled by the Gingerbread Man, John Dough, with Chick the Cherub as his Prime Minister. The Hawk merely stopped here long enough to rest, and then he flew north and passed over a fine country called Merryland, which is ruled by a lovely Wax Doll. Then, following the curve of the Desert, he turned north and settled on a tree-top in the Kingdom of Noland.

Kiki was tired by this time, and the sun was now setting, so he decided to remain here till morning. From his tree-top he could see a house near by, which looked very comfortable. A man was milking a cow in the yard and a pleasant-faced woman came to the door and called him to supper.

That made Kiki wonder what sort of food hawks ate. He felt hungry, but didn't know what to eat or where to get it. Also he thought a bed would be more comfortable than a tree-top for sleeping, so he hopped to the ground and said: "I want to become Kiki Aru again—**Pyrzqxgl!**"

Instantly he had resumed his natural shape, and going to the house, he knocked upon the door and asked for some supper.

"Who are you?" asked the man of the house.

"A stranger from the Land of Oz," replied Kiki Aru.

28

Chapter Two

"Then you are welcome," said the man.

Kiki was given a good supper and a good bed, and he behaved very well, although he refused to answer all the questions the good people of Noland asked him. Having escaped from his home and found a way to see the world, the young man was no longer unhappy, and so he was no longer cross and disagreeable. The people thought him a very respectable person and gave him breakfast next morning, after which he started on his way feeling quite contented.

Having walked for an hour or two through the pretty country that is ruled by King Bud, Kiki Aru decided he could travel faster and see more as a bird, so he transformed himself into a white dove and visited the great city of Nole and saw the King's palace and gardens and many other places of interest. Then he flew westward into the Kingdom of Ix, and after a day in Queen Zixi's country went on westward into the Land of Ev. Every place he visited he thought was much more pleasant than the saucer-country of the Hyups, and he decided that when he reached the finest country of all he would settle there and enjoy his future life to the utmost.

In the Land of Ev he resumed his own shape again, for the cities and villages were close together and he

The Magic of Oz

could easily go on foot from one to another of them.

Toward evening he came to a good Inn and asked the inn-keeper if he could have food and lodging.

"You can if you have the money to pay," said the man, "otherwise you must go elsewhere."

This surprised Kiki, for in the Land of Oz they do not use money at all, everyone being allowed to take what he wishes without price. He had no money, therefore, and so he turned away to seek hospitality elsewhere. Looking through an open window into one of the rooms of the Inn, as he passed along, he saw an old man counting on a table a big heap of gold pieces, which Kiki thought to be money. One of these would buy him supper and a bed, he reflected, so he transformed himself into a magpie and, flying through the open window, caught up one of the gold pieces in his beak and flew out again before the old man could interfere. Indeed, the old man who was robbed was quite helpless, for he dared not leave his pile of gold to chase the magpie, and before he could place the gold in a sack and the sack in his pocket the robber bird was out of sight and to seek it would be folly.

Kiki Aru flew to a group of trees and, dropping the gold piece to the ground, resumed his proper shape, and then picked up the money and put it in his pocket.

"You'll be sorry for this!" exclaimed a small voice just over his head.

Kiki looked up and saw that a sparrow, perched upon a branch, was watching him.

"Sorry for what?" he demanded.

"Oh, I saw the whole thing," asserted the sparrow. "I saw you look in the window at the gold, and then make yourself into a magpie and rob the poor man, and then I saw you fly here and make the bird into your former shape. That's magic, and magic is wicked

and unlawful; and you stole money, and that's a still greater crime. You'll be sorry, some day."

"I don't care," replied Kiki Aru, scowling.

"Aren't you afraid to be wicked?" asked the sparrow.

"No, I didn't know I was being wicked," said Kiki, "but if I was, I'm glad of it. I hate good people. I've always wanted to be wicked, but I didn't know how."

"Haw, haw, haw!" laughed someone behind him, in a big voice; "that's the proper spirit, my lad! I'm glad I've met you; shake hands."

The sparrow gave a frightened squeak and flew away.

Two Bad Ones

CHAPTER 3

Kiki turned around and saw a queer old man standing near. He didn't stand straight, for he was crooked. He had a fat body and thin legs and arms. He had a big, round face with bushy, white whiskers that came to a point below his waist, and white hair that came to a point on top of his head. He wore dull-gray clothes that were tight fitting, and his pockets were all bunched out as if stuffed full of something.

"I didn't know you were here," said Kiki.

"I didn't come until after you did," said the queer old man.

"Who are you?" asked Kiki.

"My name's Ruggedo. I used to be the Nome King; but I got kicked out of my country, and now I'm a wanderer."

"What made them kick you out?" inquired the Hyup boy.

"Well, it's the fashion to kick kings nowadays. I was a pretty good King — to myself — but those dreadful Oz people wouldn't let me alone. So I had to abdicate."

"What does that mean?"

"It means to be kicked out. But let's talk about something pleasant. Who are you and where did you come from?"

"I'm called Kiki Aru. I used to live on Mount Munch in the Land of Oz, but now I'm a wanderer like yourself."

The Nome King gave him a shrewd look.

"I heard that bird say that you transformed yourself into a magpie and back again. Is that true?"

Kiki hesitated, but saw no reason to deny it. He

felt that it would make him appear more important.

"Well — yes," he said.

"Then you're a wizard?"

"No; I only understand transformations," he admitted.

"Well, that's pretty good magic, anyhow," declared old Ruggedo. "I used to have some very fine magic, myself, but my enemies took it all away from me. Where are you going now?"

"I'm going into the inn, to get some supper and a bed," said Kiki.

"Have you the money to pay for it?" asked the Nome.

"I have one gold piece."

"Which you stole. Very good. And you're glad that you're wicked. Better yet. I like you, young man, and I'll go to the inn with you if you'll promise not to eat eggs for supper."

"Don't you like eggs?" asked Kiki.

"I'm afraid of 'em; they're dangerous!" said Ruggedo, with a shudder.

"All right," agreed Kiki; "I won't ask for eggs."

"Then come along," said the Nome.

When they entered the inn, the landlord scowled at Kiki and said:

Chapter Three

"I told you I would not feed you unless you had money."

Kiki showed him the gold piece.

"And how about you?" asked the landlord, turning to Ruggedo. "Have you money?"

"I've something better," answered the old Nome, and taking a bag from one of his pockets he poured from it upon the table a mass of glittering gems — diamonds, rubies and emeralds.

The landlord was very polite to the strangers after that. He served them an excellent supper, and while they ate it, the Hyup boy asked his companion:

"Where did you get so many jewels?"

"Well, I'll tell you," answered the Nome. "When those Oz people took my kingdom away from me — just because it was my kingdom and I wanted to run it to suit myself — they said I could take as many precious stones as I could carry. So I had a lot of pockets made in my clothes and loaded them all up. Jewels are fine things to have with you when you travel; you can trade them for anything."

"Are they better than gold pieces?" asked Kiki.

"The smallest of these jewels is worth a hundred gold pieces such as you stole from the old man."

The Magic of Oz

"Don't talk so loud," begged Kiki, uneasily. "Some one else might hear what you are saying."

After supper they took a walk together, and the former Nome King said:

"Do you know the Shaggy Man, and the Scarecrow, and the Tin Woodman, and Dorothy, and Ozma and all the other Oz people?"

"No," replied the boy, "I have never been away from Mount Munch until I flew over the Deadly Desert the other day in the shape of a hawk."

"Then you've never seen the Emerald City of Oz?"

"Never."

"Well," said the Nome, "I knew all the Oz people, and you can guess I do not love them. All during my wanderings I have brooded on how I can be revenged on them. Now that I've met you I can see a way to conquer the Land of Oz and be King there myself, which is better than being King of the Nomes."

"How can you do that?" inquired Kiki Aru, wonderingly.

"Never mind how. In the first place, I'll make a bargain with you. Tell me the secret of how to perform transformations and I will give you a pocketful of jewels, the biggest and finest that I possess."

"No," said Kiki, who realized that to share his

power with another would be dangerous to himself.

"I'll give you *two* pocketsful of jewels," said the Nome.

"No;" answered Kiki.

"I'll give you every jewel I possess."

"No, no, no!" said Kiki, who was beginning to be frightened.

"Then," said the Nome, with a wicked look at the boy, "I'll tell the inn-keeper that you stole that gold piece and he will have you put in prison."

Kiki laughed at the threat.

"Before he can do that," said he, "I will transform myself into a lion and tear him to pieces, or into a bear and eat him up, or into a fly and fly away where he could not find me."

"Can you really do such wonderful transformations?" asked the old Nome, looking at his curiously.

"Of course," declared Kiki. "I can transform you into a stick of wood, in a flash, or into a stone, and leave you here by the roadside."

The wicked Nome shivered a little when he heard that, but it made him long more than ever to possess the great secret. After a while he said:

"I'll tell you what I'll do. If you will help me to conquer Oz and to transform the Oz people, who are my enemies, into sticks or stones, by telling me your secret, I'll agree to make *you* the Ruler of all Oz, and I will be your Prime Minister and see that your orders are obeyed."

"I'll help do that," said Kiki, "but I won't tell you my secret."

The Nome was so furious at this refusal that he jumped up and down with rage and spluttered and choked for a long time before he could control his passion. But the boy was not at all frightened. He laughed at the wicked old Nome, which made him more furious than ever.

"Let's give up the idea," he proposed, when Ruggedo had quieted somewhat. "I don't know the Oz people you mention and so they are not my enemies. If they've kicked you out of your kingdom, that's your affair — not mine."

"Wouldn't you like to be king of that splendid fairyland?" asked Ruggedo.

"Yes, I would," replied Kiki Aru; "but you want to be king yourself, and we would quarrel over it."

"No," said the Nome, trying to deceive him. "I don't care to be king of Oz, come to think it over. I don't even care to live in that country. What I want first is revenge. If we can conquer Oz, I'll get enough magic then to conquer my own kingdom of the Nomes, and I'll go back and live in my underground caverns, which are more home-like than the top of the earth. So here's my proposition: Help me conquer Oz and get revenge, and help me get the magic away from

Glinda and the Wizard, and I'll let you be King of Oz forever afterward."

"I'll think it over," answered Kiki, and that is all he would say that evening.

In the night when all in the Inn were asleep but

The Magic of Oz

himself, old Ruggedo the Nome, rose softly from his couch and went into the room of Kiki Aru the Hyup, and searched everywhere for the magic tool that performed his transformations. Of course, there was no such tool, and although Ruggedo searched in all the boy's pockets, he found nothing magical whatever. So he went back to his bed and began to doubt that Kiki could perform transformations.

Next morning he said:

"Which way do you travel to-day?"

"I think I shall visit the Rose Kingdom," answered the boy.

"That is a long journey," declared the Nome.

"I shall transform myself into a bird," said Kiki, "and so fly to the Rose Kingdom in an hour."

"Then transform me, also, into a bird, and I will go with you," suggested Ruggedo. "But, in that case, let us fly together to the Land of Oz, and see what it looks like."

Kiki thought this over. Pleasant as were the countries he had visited, he heard everywhere that the Land of Oz was more beautiful and delightful. The Land of Oz was his own country, too, and if there was any possibility of his becoming its King, he must know something about it.

Chapter Three

While Kiki the Hyup thought, Ruggedo the Nome was also thinking. This boy possessed a marvelous power, and although very simple in some ways, he was determined not to part with his secret. However, if Ruggedo could get him to transport the wily old Nome to Oz, which he could reach in no other way, he might then induce the boy to follow his advice and enter into the plot for revenge, which he had already planned in his wicked heart.

"There are wizards and magicians in Oz," remarked Kiki, after a time. "They might discover us, in spite of our transformations."

"Not if we are careful," Ruggedo assured him. "Ozma has a Magic Picture, in which she can see whatever she wishes to see; but Ozma will know nothing of our going to Oz, and so she will not command her Magic Picture to show where we are or what we are doing. Glinda the Good has a Great Book called the Book of Records, in which is magically written everything that people do in the Land of Oz, just the instant they do it."

"Then," said Kiki, "there is no use our attempting to conquer the country, for Glinda would read in her book all that we do, and as her magic is greater than mine, she would soon put a stop to our plans."

The Magic of Oz

"I said 'people,' didn't I?" retorted the Nome. "The book doesn't make a record of what birds do, or beasts. It only tells the doings of people. So, if we fly into the country as birds, Glinda won't know anything about it."

"Two birds couldn't conquer the Land of Oz," asserted the boy, scornfully.

"No; that's true," admitted Ruggedo, and then he rubbed his forehead and stroked his long pointed beard and thought some more.

"Ah, now I have the idea!" he declared. "I sup-

44

pose you can transform us into beasts as well as birds?"

"Of course."

"And can you make a bird a beast, and a beast a bird again, without taking a human form in between?"

"Certainly," said Kiki. "I can transform myself or others into anything that can talk. There's a magic word that must be spoken in connection with the transformations, and as beasts and birds and dragons and fishes can talk in Oz, we may become any of these we desire to. However, if I transformed myself into a tree, I would always remain a tree, because then I could not utter the magic word to change the transformation."

"I see; I see," said Ruggedo, nodding his bushy, white head until the point of his hair waved back and forth like a pendulum. "That fits in with my idea, exactly. Now, listen, and I'll explain to you my plan. We'll fly to Oz as birds and settle in one of the thick forests in the Gillikin Country. There you will transform us into powerful beasts, and as Glinda doesn't keep any track of the doings of beasts we can act without being discovered."

"But how can two beasts raise an army to conquer the powerful people of Oz?" inquired Kiki.

The Magic of Oz

"That's easy. But not an army of *people*, mind you. That would be quickly discovered. And while we are in Oz you and I will never resume our human forms until we've conquered the country and destroyed Glinda, and Ozma, and the Wizard, and Dorothy, and all the rest, and so have nothing more to fear from them."

"It is impossible to kill anyone in the Land of Oz," declared Kiki.

"It isn't necessary to kill the Oz people," rejoined Ruggedo.

"I'm afraid I don't understand you," objected the boy. "What will happen to the Oz people, and what sort of an army could we get together, except of people?"

"I'll tell you. The forests of Oz are full of beasts. Some of them, in the far-away places, are savage and cruel, and would gladly follow a leader as savage as themselves. They have never troubled the Oz people much, because they had no leader to urge them on, but we will tell them to help us conquer Oz and as a reward we will transform all the beasts into men and women, and let them live in the houses and enjoy all the good things; and we will transform all the people of Oz into beasts of various sorts, and send

46

them to live in the forests and the jungles. That is a splendid idea, you must admit, and it's so easy that we won't have any trouble at all to carry it through to success."

"Will the beasts consent, do you think?" asked the boy.

"To be sure they will. We can get every beast in Oz on our side — except a few who live in Ozma's palace, and they won't count."

Conspirators

CHAPTER 4

Kiki Aru didn't know much about Oz and didn't know much about the beasts who lived there, but the old Nome's plan seemed to him to be quite reasonable. He had a faint suspicion that Ruggedo meant to get the best of him in some way, and he resolved to keep a close watch on his fellow-conspirator. As long as he kept to himself the secret word of the transfor-

mations, Ruggedo would not dare to harm him, and he promised himself that as soon as they had conquered Oz, he would transform the old Nome into a marble statue and keep him in that form forever.

Ruggedo, on his part, decided that he could, by careful watching and listening, surprise the boy's secret, and when he had learned the magic word he would transform Kiki Aru into a bundle of faggots and burn him up and so be rid of him.

This is always the way with wicked people. They cannot be trusted even by one another. Ruggedo thought he was fooling Kiki, and Kiki thought he was fooling Ruggedo; so both were pleased.

"It's a long way across the Desert," remarked the boy, "and the sands are hot and send up poisonous vapors. Let us wait until evening and then fly across in the night when it will be cooler."

The former Nome King agreed to this, and the two spent the rest of that day in talking over their plans. When evening came they paid the inn-keeper and walked out to a little grove of trees that stood near by.

"Remain here for a few minutes and I'll soon be back," said Kiki, and walking swiftly away, he left the Nome standing in the grove. Ruggedo wondered where he had gone, but stood quietly in his place until,

The Magic of Oz

all of a sudden, his form changed to that of a great eagle, and he uttered a piercing cry of astonishment and flapped his wings in a sort of panic. At once his eagle cry was answered from beyond the grove, and another eagle, even larger and more powerful than the transformed Ruggedo, came sailing through the trees and alighted beside him.

"Now we are ready for the start," said the voice of Kiki, coming from the eagle.

Ruggedo realized that this time he had been outwitted. He had thought Kiki would utter the magic word in his presence, and so he would learn what it was, but the boy had been too shrewd for that.

As the two eagles mounted high into the air and began their flight across the great Desert that separates the Land of Oz from all the rest of the world, the Nome said:

"When I was king of the Nomes I had a magic way of working transformations that I thought was good, but it could not compare with your secret word. I had to have certain tools and make passes and say a lot of mystic words before I could transform anybody."

"What became of your magic tools?" inquired Kiki.

"The Oz people took them all away from me — that horrid girl, Dorothy, and that terrible fairy, Ozma,

The Magic of Oz

the Ruler of Oz — at the time they took away my underground kingdom and kicked me upstairs into the cold, heartless world."

"Why did you let them do that?" asked the boy.

"Well," said Ruggedo, "I couldn't help it. They

rolled eggs at me — *eggs* — dreadful eggs! — and if an egg even touches a Nome, he is ruined for life."

"Is any kind of an egg dangerous to a Nome?"

"Any kind and every kind. An egg is the only thing I'm afraid of."

A Happy Corner of Oz

CHAPTER 5

There is no other country so beautiful as the Land of Oz. There are no other people so happy and contented and prosperous as the Oz people. They have all they desire; they love and admire their beautiful girl Ruler, Ozma of Oz, and they mix work and play so justly that both are delightful and satisfying and no one has any reason to complain. Once in a while

The Magic of Oz

something happens in Oz to disturb the people's happiness for a brief time, for so rich and attractive a fairyland is sure to make a few selfish and greedy outsiders envious, and therefore certain evil-doers have treacherously plotted to conquer Oz and enslave its people and destroy its girl Ruler, and so gain the wealth of Oz for themselves. But up to the time when the cruel and crafty Nome, Ruggedo, conspired with Kiki Aru, the Hyup, all such attempts had failed. The Oz people suspected no danger. Life in the world's nicest fairyland was one round of joyous, happy days.

In the center of the Emerald City of Oz, the capital city of Ozma's dominions, is a vast and beautiful garden, surrounded by a wall inlaid with shining emeralds, and in the center of this garden stands Ozma's Royal Palace, the most splendid building ever constructed. From a hundred towers and domes floated the banners of Oz, which included the Ozmies, the Munchkins, the Gillikins, the Winkies and the Quadlings. The banner of the Munchkins is blue, that of the Winkies yellow; the Gillikin banner is purple, and the Quadling's banner is red. The colors of the Emerald City are of course green. Ozma's own banner has a green center, and is divided into four quarters. These quarters are colored blue, purple, yellow and red, indicating that she rules over all the countries of the Land of Oz.

This fairyland is so big, however, that all of it is not yet known to its girl Ruler, and it is said that in some far parts of the country, in forests and mountain fastnesses, in hidden valleys and thick jungles, are people and beasts that know as little about Ozma as she knows of them. Still, these unknown subjects are not nearly so numerous as the known inhabitants of Oz, who occupy all the countries near to the Emerald City. Indeed, I'm sure it will not be long until all parts of the fairyland of Oz are explored and their peoples made acquainted with their Ruler, for in Ozma's palace are several of her friends who are so curious that they are constantly discovering new and extraordinary places and inhabitants.

One of the most frequent discoverers of these hidden places in Oz is a little Kansas girl named Dorothy, who is Ozma's dearest friend and lives in luxurious rooms in the Royal Palace. Dorothy is, indeed, a Princess of Oz, but she does not like to be called a princess, and because she is simple and sweet and does not pretend to be anything but an ordinary little girl, she is called just " Dorothy " by everybody and is the

The Magic of Oz

most popular person, next to Ozma, in all the Land of Oz.

One morning Dorothy crossed the hall of the palace and knocked on the door of another girl named Trot, also a guest and friend of Ozma. When told to enter,

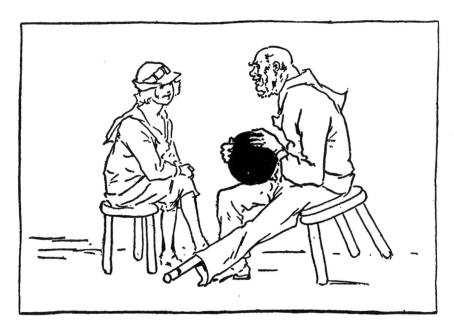

Dorothy found that Trot had company, an old sailor-man with one wooden leg and one meat leg, who was sitting by the open window puffing smoke from a corn-cob pipe. This sailor-man was named Cap'n Bill, and he had accompanied Trot to the Land of Oz and

was her oldest and most faithful comrade and friend. Dorothy liked Cap'n Bill, too, and after she had greeted him, she said to Trot:

"You know, Ozma's birthday is next month, and I've been wondering what I can give her as a birthday present. She's so good to us all that we certainly ought to remember her birthday."

"That's true," agreed Trot. "I've been wondering, too, what I could give Ozma. It's pretty hard to decide, 'cause she's got already all she wants, and as she's a fairy and knows a lot about magic, she could satisfy any wish."

"I know," returned Dorothy, "but that isn't the point. It isn't that Ozma *needs* anything, but that it will please her to know we've remembered her birthday. But what shall we give her?"

Trot shook her head in despair.

"I've tried to think and I can't," she declared.

"It's the same way with me," said Dorothy.

"I know one thing that 'ud please her," remarked Cap'n Bill, turning his round face with its fringe of whiskers toward the two girls and staring at them with his big, light-blue eyes wide open.

"What is it, Cap'n Bill?"

"It's an Enchanted Flower," said he. "It's a pretty

plant that stands in a golden flower-pot an' grows all sorts o' flowers, one after another. One minute a fine rose buds an' blooms, an' then a tulip, an' next a chrys — chrys — "

" — anthemum," said Dorothy, helping him.

" That's it; and next a dahlia, an' then a daffydil, an' on all through the range o' posies. Jus' as soon as one fades away, another comes, of a different sort, an' the perfume from 'em is mighty snifty, an' they keeps bloomin' night and day, year in an' year out."

" That's wonderful! " exclaimed Dorothy. " I think Ozma would like it."

" But where is the Magic Flower, and how can we get it? " asked Trot.

" Dun'no, zac'ly," slowly replied Cap'n Bill. " The Glass Cat tol' me about it only yesterday, an' said it was in some lonely place up at the nor'east o' here. The Glass Cat goes travelin' all around Oz, you know, an' the little critter sees a lot o' things no one else does."

" That's true," said Dorothy, thoughtfully. " Northeast of here must be in the Munchkin Country, and perhaps a good way off, so let's ask the Glass Cat to tell us how to get to the Magic Flower."

So the two girls, with Cap'n Bill stumping along on

his wooden leg after them, went out into the garden, and after some time spent in searching, they found the Glass Cat curled up in the sunshine beside a bush, fast asleep.

The Glass Cat is one of the most curious creatures

in all Oz. It was made by a famous magician named Dr. Pipt before Ozma had forbidden her subjects to work magic. Dr. Pipt had made the Glass Cat to catch mice, but the Cat refused to catch mice and was considered more curious than useful.

59

The Magic of Oz

This astonishing cat was made all of glass and was so clear and transparent that you could see through it as easily as through a window. In the top of its head, however, was a mass of delicate pink balls which looked like jewels but were intended for brains. It had a heart made of a blood-red ruby. The eyes were two large emeralds. But, aside from these colors, all the rest of the animal was of clear glass, and it had a spun-glass tail that was really beautiful.

"Here, wake up," said Cap'n Bill. "We want to talk to you."

Slowly the Glass Cat got upon its feet, yawned and then looked at the three who stood before it.

"How dare you disturb me?" it asked in a peevish voice. "You ought to be ashamed of yourselves."

"Never mind that," returned the Sailor. "Do you remember tellin' me yesterday 'bout a Magic Flower in a Gold Pot?"

"Do you think I'm a fool? Look at my brains — you can see 'em work. Of course I remember!" said the cat.

"Well, where can we find it?"

"You can't. It's none of your business, anyhow. Go away and let me sleep," advised the Glass Cat.

"Now, see here," said Dorothy; "we want the Magic

Flower to give to Ozma on her birthday. You'd be glad to please Ozma, wouldn't you?"

"I'm not sure," replied the creature. "Why should I want to please anybody?"

"You've got a heart, 'cause I can see it inside of you," said Trot.

"Yes; it's a pretty heart, and I'm fond of it," said the cat, twisting around to view its own body. "But it's made from a ruby, and it's hard as nails."

"Aren't you good for *any*thing?" asked Trot.

The Magic of Oz

"Yes, I'm pretty to look at, and that's more than can be said of you," retorted the creature.

Trot laughed at this, and Dorothy, who understood the Glass Cat pretty well, said soothingly:

"You are indeed beautiful, and if you can tell Cap'n Bill where to find the Magic Flower, all the people in Oz will praise your cleverness. The Flower will belong to Ozma, but everyone will know the Glass Cat discovered it."

This was the kind of praise the crystal creature liked.

"Well," it said, while the pink brains rolled around, "I found the Magic Flower way up in the north of the Munchkin Country where few people live or ever go. There's a river there that flows through a forest, and in the middle of the river in the middle of the forest there is a small island on which stands the gold pot in which grows the Magic Flower."

"How did you get to the island?" asked Dorothy. "Glass cats can't swim."

"No, but I'm not afraid of water," was the reply. "I just walked across the river on the bottom."

"Under the water?" exclaimed Trot.

The cat gave her a scornful look.

"How could I walk *over* the water on the *bottom*

of the river? If you were transparent, anyone could see *your* brains were not working. But I'm sure you could never find the place alone. It has always been hidden from the Oz people."

"But you, with your fine pink brains, could find it again, I s'pose," remarked Dorothy.

"Yes; and if you want that Magic Flower for Ozma, I'll go with you and show you the way."

"That's lovely of you!" declared Dorothy. "Trot

and Cap'n Bill will go with you, for this is to be their birthday present to Ozma. While you're gone I'll have to find something else to give her."

"All right. Come on, then, Cap'n," said the Glass Cat, starting to move away.

"Wait a minute," begged Trot. "How long will we be gone?"

"Oh, about a week."

"Then I'll put some things in a basket to take with us," said the girl, and ran into the palace to make her preparations for the journey.

Ozma's Birthday Presents

CHAPTER 6

When Cap'n Bill and Trot and the Glass Cat had started for the hidden island in the far-off river to get the Magic Flower, Dorothy wondered again what she could give Ozma on her birthday. She met the Patchwork Girl and said:

"What are you going to give Ozma for a birthday present?"

"I've written a song for

her," answered the strange Patchwork Girl, who went by the name of "Scraps," and who, though stuffed with cotton, had a fair assortment of mixed brains. "It's a splendid song and the chorus runs this way:

> "I am crazy;
>   You're a daisy,
>   Ozma dear;
>   I'm demented;
>   You're contented,
>   Ozma dear;
> I am patched and gay and glary;
> You're a sweet and lovely fairy;
> May your birthdays all be happy,
>   Ozma dear!"

"How do you like it, Dorothy?" inquired the Patchwork Girl.

"Is it good poetry, Scraps?" asked Dorothy, doubtfully.

"It's as good as any ordinary song," was the reply. "I have given it a dandy title, too. I shall call the song: 'When Ozma Has a Birthday, Everybody's Sure to Be Gay, for She Cannot Help the Fact That She Was Born.'"

"That's a pretty long title, Scraps," said Dorothy.

"That makes it stylish," replied the Patchwork Girl, turning a somersault and alighting on one stuffed foot. "Now-a-days the titles are sometimes longer than the songs."

Dorothy left her and walked slowly toward the palace, where she met the Tin Woodman just going up the front steps.

"What are you going to give Ozma on her birthday?" she asked.

The Magic of Oz

"It's a secret, but I'll tell you," replied the Tin Woodman, who was Emperor of the Winkies. "I am having my people make Ozma a lovely girdle set with beautiful tin nuggets. Each tin nugget will be surrounded by a circle of emeralds, just to set it off to good advantage. The clasp of the girdle will be pure tin! Won't that be fine?"

"I'm sure she'll like it," said Dorothy. "Do you know what *I* can give her?"

"I haven't the slightest idea, Dorothy. It took me three months to think of my own present for Ozma."

The girl walked thoughtfully around to the back of the palace, and presently came upon the famous Scarecrow of Oz, who was having two of the palace servants stuff his legs with fresh straw.

"What are you going to give Ozma on her birthday?" asked Dorothy.

"I want to surprise her," answered the Scarecrow.

"I won't tell," promised Dorothy.

"Well, I'm having some straw slippers made for her — all straw, mind you, and braided very artistically. Ozma has always admired my straw filling, so I'm sure she'll be pleased with these lovely straw slippers."

"Ozma will be pleased with anything her loving

friends give her," said the girl. "What *I'm* worried about, Scarecrow, is what to give Ozma that she hasn't got already."

"That's what worried me, until I thought of the slippers," said the Scarecrow. "You'll have to *think,*

Dorothy; that's the only way to get a good idea. If I hadn't such wonderful brains, I'd never have thought of those straw foot-decorations."

Dorothy left him and went to her room, where she sat down and tried to think hard. A Pink Kitten was

The Magic of Oz

curled up on the window-sill and Dorothy asked her:

"What can I give Ozma for her birthday present?"

"Oh, give her some milk," replied the Pink Kitten; "that's the nicest thing I know of."

A fuzzy little black dog had squatted down at Dorothy's feet and now looked up at her with intelligent eyes.

"Tell me, Toto," said the girl; "what would Ozma like best for a birthday present?"

The little black dog wagged his tail.

"Your love," said he. "Ozma wants to be loved more than anything else."

"But I already love her, Toto!"

"Then tell her you love her twice as much as you ever did before."

"That wouldn't be true," objected Dorothy, "for I've always loved her as much as I could, and, really, Toto, I want to give Ozma some *present,* 'cause everyone else will give her a present."

"Let me see," said Toto. "How would it be to give her that useless Pink Kitten?"

"No, Toto; that wouldn't do."

"Then six kisses."

"No; that's no present."

"Well, I guess you'll have to figure it out for yourself, Dorothy," said the little dog. "To *my* notion you're more particular than Ozma will be."

Dorothy decided that if anyone could help her it would be Glinda the Good, the wonderful Sorceress

of Oz who was Ozma's faithful subject and friend. But Glinda's castle was in the Quadling Country and quite a journey from the Emerald City.

So the little girl went to Ozma and asked permission to use the Wooden Sawhorse and the royal Red Wagon

The Magic of Oz

to pay a visit to Glinda, and the girl Ruler kissed Princess Dorothy and graciously granted permission.

The Wooden Sawhorse was one of the most remarkable creatures in Oz. Its body was a small log and its legs were limbs of trees stuck in the body. Its eyes were knots, its mouth was sawed in the end of the log and its ears were two chips. A small branch had been left at the rear end of the log to serve as a tail.

Ozma herself, during one of her early adventures, had brought this wooden horse to life, and so she was much attached to the queer animal and had shod the bottoms of its wooden legs with plates of gold so they would not wear out. The sawhorse was a swift and willing traveler, and though it could talk if need arose, it seldom said anything unless spoken to. When the Sawhorse was harnessed to the Red Wagon there were no reins to guide him because all that was needed was to tell him where to go.

Dorothy now told him to go to Glinda's Castle and the Sawhorse carried her there with marvelous speed.

" Glinda," said Dorothy, when she had been greeted by the Sorceress, who was tall and stately, with handsome and dignified features and dressed in a splendid and becoming gown, " what are you going to give Ozma for a birthday present? "

The Sorceress smiled and answered:

" Come into my patio* and I will show you."

So they entered a place that was surrounded by the wings of the great castle but had no roof, and was

filled with flowers and fountains and exquisite statuary and many settees and chairs of polished marble or filigree gold. Here there were gathered fifty beautiful young girls, Glinda's handmaids, who had been selected from all parts of the Land of Oz on account

* Pronounced *pa'-shi-o*.

of their wit and beauty and sweet dispositions. It was a great honor to be made one of Glinda's handmaidens.

When Dorothy followed the Sorceress into this delightful patio all the fifty girls were busily weaving, and their shuttles were filled with a sparkling green spun glass such as the little girl had never seen before.

"What is it, Glinda?" she asked.

"One of my recent discoveries," explained the Sorceress. "I have found a way to make threads from emeralds, by softening the stones and then spinning them into long, silken strands. With these emerald threads we are weaving cloth to make Ozma a splendid court gown for her birthday. You will notice that the threads have all the beautiful glitter and luster of the emeralds from which they are made, and so Ozma's new dress will be the most magnificent the world has ever seen, and quite fitting for our lovely Ruler of the Fairyland of Oz."

Dorothy's eyes were fairly dazed by the brilliance of the emerald cloth, some of which the girls had already woven.

"I've never seen *any*thing so beautiful!" she said, with a sigh. "But tell me, Glinda, what can *I* give our lovely Ozma on her birthday?"

Chapter Six

The good Sorceress considered this question for a long time before she replied. Finally she said:

"Of course there will be a grand feast at the Royal Palace on Ozma's birthday, and all our friends will be present. So I suggest that you make a fine big birthday cake for Ozma, and surround it with candles."

"Oh, just a *cake!*" exclaimed Dorothy, in disappointment.

"Nothing is nicer for a birthday," said the Sorceress.

"How many candles should there be on the cake?" asked the girl.

"Just a row of them," replied Glinda, "for no one knows how old Ozma is, although she appears to us to be just a young girl — as fresh and fair as if she had lived but a few years."

"A cake doesn't seem like much of a present," Dorothy asserted.

"Make it a surprise cake," suggested the Sorceress. "Don't you remember the four and twenty blackbirds that were baked in a pie? Well, you need not use live blackbirds in your cake, but you could have some surprise of a different sort."

"Like what?" questioned Dorothy, eagerly.

"If I told you, it wouldn't be *your* present to Ozma,

75

The Magic of Oz

but *mine,*" answered the Sorceress, with a smile. "Think it over, my dear, and I am sure you can originate a surprise that will add greatly to the joy and merriment of Ozma's birthday banquet."

Dorothy thanked her friend and entered the Red Wagon and told the Sawhorse to take her back home to the palace in the Emerald City.

On the way she thought the matter over seriously of making a surprise birthday cake and finally decided what to do.

As soon as she reached home, she went to the Wizard of Oz, who had a room fitted up in one of the high towers of the palace, where he studied magic so as to be able to perform such wizardry as Ozma commanded him to do for the welfare of her subjects.

The Wizard and Dorothy were firm friends and had enjoyed many strange adventures together. He was a little man with a bald head and sharp eyes and a round, jolly face, and because he was neither haughty nor proud he had become a great favorite with the Oz people.

"Wizard," said Dorothy, "I want you to help me fix up a present for Ozma's birthday."

"I'll be glad to do anything for you and for Ozma," he answered. "What's on your mind, Dorothy?"

"I'm going to make a great cake, with frosting and candles, and all that, you know."

"Very good," said the Wizard.

"In the center of this cake I'm going to leave a

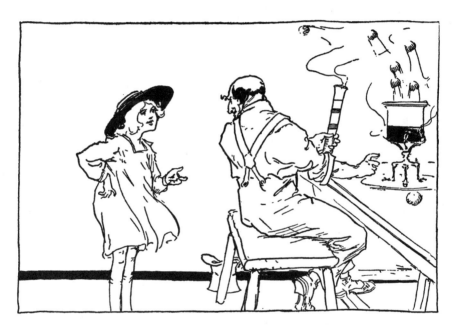

hollow place, with just a roof of the frosting over it," continued the girl.

"Very good," repeated the Wizard, nodding his bald head.

"In that hollow place," said Dorothy, "I want to hide a lot of monkeys about three inches high, and after the cake is placed on the banquet table, I want the monkeys to break through the frosting and dance around on the table-cloth. Then, I want each monkey to cut out a piece of cake and hand it to a guest."

"Mercy me!" cried the little Wizard, as he chuckled with laughter. "Is that *all* you want, Dorothy?"

"Almost," said she. "Can you think of anything more the little monkeys can do, Wizard?"

"Not just now," he replied. "But where will you get such tiny monkeys?"

"That's where you're to help me," said Dorothy. "In some of those wild forests in the Gillikin Country are lots of monkeys."

"Big ones," said the Wizard.

"Well, you and I will go there, and we'll get some of the big monkeys, and you will make them small — just three inches high — by means of your magic, and we'll put the little monkeys all in a basket and bring them home with us. Then you'll train them to dance — up here in your room, where no one can see them — and on Ozma's birthday we'll put 'em into the cake and they'll know by that time just what to do."

The Wizard looked at Dorothy with admiring approval, and chuckled again.

"That's really clever, my dear," he said, "and I see

no reason why we can't do it, just the way you say, if only we can get the wild monkeys to agree to it."

"Do you think they'll object?" asked the girl.

"Yes; but perhaps we can argue them into it. Anyhow, it's worth trying, and I'll help you if you'll agree to let this Surprise Cake be a present to Ozma from you and me together. I've been wondering what *I* could give Ozma, and as I've got to train the monkeys as well as make them small, I think you ought to make me your partner."

"Of course," said Dorothy; "I'll be glad to do so."

"Then, it's a bargain," declared the Wizard. "We must go to seek those monkeys at once, however, for it will take time to train them and we'll have to travel a good way to the Gillikin forests where they live."

"I'm ready to go any time," agreed Dorothy. "Shall we ask Ozma to let us take the Sawhorse?"

The Wizard did not answer that at once. He took time to think of the suggestion.

"No," he answered at length, "the Red Wagon couldn't get through the thick forests and there's some danger to us in going into the wild places to search for monkeys. So I propose we take the Cowardly Lion and the Hungry Tiger. We can ride on their backs as well as in the Red Wagon, and if there is danger to us from other beasts, these two friendly champions will protect us from all harm."

"That's a splendid idea!" exclaimed Dorothy. "Let's go now and ask the Hungry Tiger and the Cowardly Lion if they will help us. Shall we ask Ozma if we can go?"

"I think not," said the Wizard, getting his hat and his black bag of magic tools. "This is to be a surprise for her birthday, and so she must n't know where we're going. We'll just leave word, in case Ozma inquires for us, that we'll be back in a few days."

The Forest of Gugu

CHAPTER 7

In the central western part of the Gillikin Country is a great tangle of trees called Gugu Forest. It is the biggest forest in all Oz and stretches miles and miles in every d i r e c t i o n — north, south, east and west. Adjoining it on the east side is a range of rugged mountains covered with underbrush and small twisted trees. You can

The Magic of Oz

find this place by looking at the Map of the Land of Oz.

Gugu Forest is the home of most of the wild beasts that inhabit Oz. These are seldom disturbed in their leafy haunts because there is no reason why Oz people should go there, except on rare occasions, and most parts of the forest have never been seen by any eyes but the eyes of the beasts who make their home there. The biggest beasts inhabit the great forest, while the smaller ones live mostly in the mountain underbrush at the east.

Now, you must know that there are laws in the forests, as well as in every other place, and these laws are made by the beasts themselves, and are necessary to keep them from fighting and tearing one another to pieces. In Gugu Forest there is a King — an enormous yellow leopard called "Gugu" — after whom the forest is named. And this King has three other beasts to advise him in keeping the laws and maintaining order — Bru the Bear, Loo the Unicorn and Rango the Gray Ape — who are known as the King's Counselors. All these are fierce and ferocious beasts, and hold their high offices because they are more intelligent and more feared than their fellows.

Since Oz became a fairyland, no man, woman or child ever dies in that land nor is anyone ever sick.

Likewise the beasts of the forests never die, so that long years add to their cunning and wisdom, as well as to their size and strength. It is possible for beasts — or even people — to be destroyed, but the task is so difficult that it is seldom attempted. Because it is free from sickness and death is one reason why Oz is a fairyland, but it is doubtful whether those who come to Oz from the outside world, as Dorothy and Button-Bright and Trot and Cap'n Bill and the Wizard did, will live forever or cannot be injured. Even Ozma is not sure about this, and so the guests of Ozma from other lands are always carefully protected from any danger, so as to be on the safe side.

In spite of the laws of the forests there are often fights among the beasts; some of them have lost an eye or an ear or even had a leg torn off. The King and the King's Counselors always punish those who start a fight, but so fierce is the nature of some beasts that they will at times fight in spite of laws and punishment.

Over this vast, wild Forest of Gugu flew two eagles, one morning, and near the center of the jungle the eagles alighted on a branch of a tall tree.

"Here is the place for us to begin our work," said one, who was Ruggedo, the Nome.

The Magic of Oz

"Do many beasts live here?" asked Kiki Aru, the other eagle.

"The forest is full of them," said the Nome. "There are enough beasts right here to enable us to conquer the people of Oz, if we can get them to consent to join us. To do that, we must go among them and tell them our plans, so we must now decide on what shapes we had better assume while in the forest."

"I suppose we must take the shapes of beasts?" said Kiki.

"Of course. But that requires some thought. All kinds of beasts live here, and a yellow leopard is King. If we become leopards, the King will be jealous of us. If we take the forms of some of the other beasts, we shall not command proper respect."

"I wonder if the beasts will attack us?" asked Kiki.

"I'm a Nome, and immortal, so nothing can hurt me," replied Ruggedo.

"I was born in the Land of Oz, so nothing can hurt me," said Kiki.

"But, in order to carry out our plans, we must win the favor of all the animals of the forest."

"Then what shall we do?" asked Kiki.

"Let us mix the shapes of several beasts, so we

will not look like any one of them," proposed the wily old Nome. "Let us have the heads of lions, the bodies of monkeys, the wings of eagles and the tails of wild asses, with knobs of gold on the end of them instead of bunches of hair."

"Won't that make a queer combination?" inquired Kiki.

"The queerer the better," declared Ruggedo.

"All right," said Kiki. "You stay here, and I'll fly away to another tree and transform us both, and then we'll climb down our trees and meet in the forest."

"No," said the Nome, "we mustn't separate. You must transform us while we are together."

"I won't do that," asserted Kiki, firmly. "You're trying to get my secret, and I won't let you."

The eyes of the other eagle flashed angrily, but Ruggedo did not dare insist. If he offended this boy, he might have to remain an eagle always and he wouldn't like that. Some day he hoped to be able to learn the secret word of the magical transformations, but just now he must let Kiki have his own way.

"All right," he said gruffly; "do as you please."

So Kiki flew to a tree that was far enough distant

so that Ruggedo could not overhear him and said: "I want Ruggedo, the Nome, and myself to have the heads of lions, the bodies of monkeys, the wings of eagles and the tails of wild asses, with knobs of gold on the ends of them instead of bunches of hair —**Pyrzqxgl!**"

He pronounced the magic word in the proper manner and at once his form changed to the one he had described. He spread his eagle's wings and finding they were strong enough to support his monkey body and lion head he flew swiftly to the tree where he had left Ruggedo. The Nome was also transformed and was climbing down the tree because the branches all around him were so thickly entwined that there was no room between them to fly.

Kiki quickly joined his comrade and it did not take them long to reach the ground.

The Li-Mon-Eags Make Trouble

CHAPTER 8

There had been trouble in the
Forest of Gugu that morning.
Chipo the Wild Boar had bit-
ten the tail off Arx the Giraffe
while the latter had his head
among the leaves of a tree,
eating his breakfast. Arx
kicked with his heels and
struck Tirrip, the great Kan-
garoo, who had a new baby
in her pouch. Tirrip knew
it was the Wild Boar's fault,

87

The Magic of Oz

so she knocked him over with one powerful blow and then ran away to escape Chipo's sharp tusks. In the chase that followed a giant porcupine stuck fifty sharp quills into the Boar and a chimpanzee in a tree threw a cocoanut at the porcupine that jammed its head into its body.

All this was against the Laws of the Forest, and when the excitement was over, Gugu the Leopard King called his royal Counselors together to decide how best to punish the offenders.

The four lords of the forest were holding solemn council in a small clearing when they saw two strange beasts approaching them — beasts the like of which they had never seen before.

Not one of the four, however, relaxed his dignity or showed by a movement that he was startled. The great Leopard crouched at full length upon a fallen tree-trunk. Bru the Bear sat on his haunches before the King; Rango the Gray Ape stood with his muscular arms folded, and Loo the Unicorn reclined, much as a horse does, between his fellow-councillors. With one consent they remained silent, eyeing with steadfast looks the intruders, who were making their way into their forest domain.

"Well met, Brothers!" said one of the strange

beasts, coming to a halt beside the group, while his comrade with hesitation lagged behind.

"We are not brothers," returned the Gray Ape, sternly. "Who are you, and how came you in the forest of Gugu?"

"We are two Li-Mon-Eags," said Ruggedo, inventing the name. "Our home is in Sky Island, and we have come to earth to warn the forest beasts that the people of Oz are about to make war upon them and enslave them, so that they will become beasts of bur-

89

The Magic of Oz

den forever after and obey only the will of their two-legged masters."

A low roar of anger arose from the Council of Beasts.

"Who's going to do that?" asked Loo the Unicorn, in a high, squeaky voice, at the same time rising to his feet.

" The people of Oz," said Ruggedo.

" But what will *we* be doing?" inquired the Unicorn.

" That's what I've come to talk to you about."

" You needn't talk! We'll fight the Oz people!" screamed the Unicorn. " We'll smash 'em; we'll trample 'em; we'll gore 'em; we'll — "

" Silence!" growled Gugu the King, and Loo obeyed, although still trembling with wrath. The cold, steady gaze of the Leopard wandered over the two strange beasts. " The people of Oz," said he, " have not been our friends; they have not been our enemies. They have let us alone, and we have let them alone. There is no reason for war between us. They have no slaves. They could not use us as slaves if they should conquer us. I think you are telling us lies, you strange Li-Mon-Eag — you mixed-up beast who are neither one thing nor another."

" Oh, on my word, it's the truth!" protested the

Nome in the beast's shape. " I wouldn't lie for the world; I — "

" Silence! " again growled Gugu the King; and, somehow, even Ruggedo was abashed and obeyed the edict.

" What do you say, Bru? " asked the king, turning to the great Bear, who had until now said nothing.

" How does the Mixed Beast know that what he says is true? " asked the Bear.

" Why, I can fly, you know, having the wings of an Eagle," explained the Nome. " I and my comrade yonder," turning to Kiki, " flew to a grove in Oz, and there we heard the people telling how they will make many ropes to snare you beasts, and then they will surround this forest, and all other forests, and make you prisoners. So we came here to warn you, for being beasts ourselves, although we live in the sky, we are your friends."

The Leopard's lip curled and showed his enormous teeth, sharp as needles. He turned to the Gray Ape.

" What do *you* think, Rango? " he asked.

" Send these mixed beasts away, your Majesty," replied the Gray Ape. " They are mischief-makers."

" Don't do that — don't do that! " cried the Unicorn, nervously. " The stranger said he would tell us what

The Magic of Oz

to do. Let him tell us, then. Are we fools, not to heed a warning?"

Gugu the King turned to Ruggedo.

"Speak, Stranger," he commanded.

"Well," said the Nome, "it's this way: The Land of Oz is a fine country. The people of Oz have many good things — houses with soft beds, all sorts of nice-tasting food, pretty clothes, lovely jewels, and many other things that beasts know nothing of. Here in the dark forests the poor beasts have hard work to get enough to eat and to find a bed to rest in. But the beasts are better than the people, and why should they not have all the good things the people have? So I propose that before the Oz people have the time to make all those ropes to snare you with, that all we beasts get together and march against the Oz people and capture them. Then the beasts will become the masters and the people their slaves."

"What good would that do us?" asked Bru the Bear.

"It would save you from slavery, for one thing, and you could enjoy all the fine things the Oz people have."

"Beasts wouldn't know what to do with the things people use," said the Gray Ape.

"But this is only part of my plan," insisted the

Nome. "Listen to the rest of it. We two Li-Mon-Eags are powerful magicians. When you have conquered the Oz people we will transform them all into beasts, and send them to the forests to live, and we will transform all the beasts into people, so they can enjoy all the wonderful delights of the Emerald City."

For a moment no beast spoke. Then the King said: "Prove it."

"Prove what?" asked Ruggedo.

"Prove that you can transform us. If you are a magician transform the Unicorn into a man. Then we will believe you. If you fail, we will destroy you."

"All right," said the Nome. "But I'm tired, so I'll let my comrade make the transformation."

Kiki Aru had stood back from the circle, but he had heard all that was said. He now realized that he must make good Ruggedo's boast, so he retreated to the edge of the clearing and whispered the magic word.

Instantly the Unicorn became a fat, chubby little man, dressed in the purple Gillikin costume, and it was hard to tell which was the more astonished, the King, the Bear, the Ape or the former Unicorn.

"It's true!" shouted the man-beast. "Good gracious, look what I am! It's wonderful!"

The Magic of Oz

The King of the Beasts now addressed Ruggedo in a more friendly tone.

"We must believe your story, since you have given us proof of your power," said he. "But why, if you are so great a magician, cannot you conquer the Oz people without our help, and so save us the trouble?"

"Alas!" replied the crafty old Nome, "no magician is able to do everything. The transformations are easy to us because we are Li-Mon-Eags, but we cannot fight, or conquer even such weak creatures as the Oz people. But we will stay with you and advise and help you, and we will transform all the Oz people into beasts, when the time comes, and all the beasts into people."

Gugu the King turned to his Counselors.

"How shall we answer this friendly stranger?" he asked.

Loo the former Unicorn was dancing around and cutting capers like a clown.

"On my word, your Majesty," he said, "this being a man is more fun than being a Unicorn."

"You look like a fool," said the Gray Ape.

"Well, I *feel* fine!" declared the man-beast.

"I think I prefer to be a Bear," said Big Bru. "I

was born a Bear, and I know a Bear's ways. So I am satisfied to live as a Bear lives."

"That," said the old Nome, "is because you know nothing better. When we have conquered the Oz people, and you become a man, you'll be glad of it."

The immense Leopard rested his chin on the log and seemed thoughtful.

"The beasts of the forest must decide this matter for themselves," he said. "Go you, Rango the Gray Ape, and tell your monkey tribe to order all the forest beasts to assemble in the Great Clearing at sunrise to-morrow. When all are gathered together, this mixed-up Beast who is a magician shall talk to them and tell them what he has told us. Then, if they decide to fight the Oz people, who have declared war on us, I will lead the beasts to battle."

Rango the Gray Ape turned at once and glided swiftly through the forest on his mission. The Bear gave a grunt and walked away. Gugu the King rose and stretched himself. Then he said to Ruggedo: "Meet us at sunrise to-morrow," and with stately stride vanished among the trees.

The man-unicorn, left alone with the strangers, suddenly stopped his foolish prancing.

"You'd better make me a Unicorn again," he said.

" I like being a man, but the forest beasts won't know I'm their friend, Loo, and they might tear me in pieces before morning."

So Kiki changed him back to his former shape, and the Unicorn departed to join his people.

Ruggedo the Nome was much pleased with his success.

" To-morrow," he said to Kiki Aru, " we'll win over these beasts and set them to fight and conquer the Oz people. Then I will have my revenge on **Ozma** and Dorothy and all the rest of my enemies."

"But I am doing all the work," said Kiki.

"Never mind; you're going to be King of Oz," promised Ruggedo.

"Will the big Leopard let me be King?" asked the boy anxiously.

The Nome came close to him and whispered:

"If Gugu the Leopard opposes us, you will transform him into a tree, and then he will be helpless."

"Of course," agreed Kiki, and he said to himself: "I shall also transform this deceitful **Nome** into **a** tree, for he lies and I cannot trust him."

The Isle of the Magic Flower

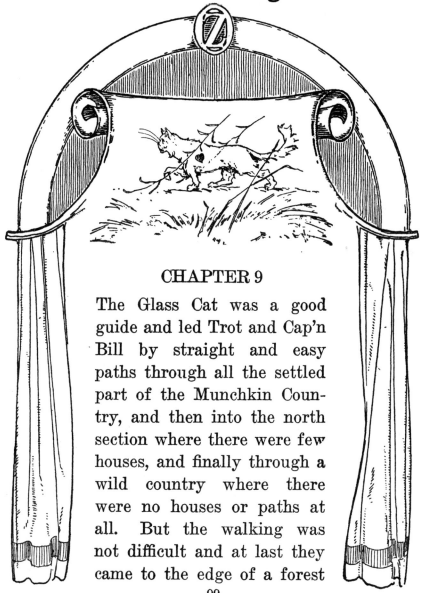

CHAPTER 9

The Glass Cat was a good guide and led Trot and Cap'n Bill by straight and easy paths through all the settled part of the Munchkin Country, and then into the north section where there were few houses, and finally through a wild country where there were no houses or paths at all. But the walking was not difficult and at last they came to the edge of a forest and stopped there to make camp and sleep until morning.

From branches of trees Cap'n Bill made a tiny house that was just big enough for the little girl to crawl into and lie down. But first they ate some of the food Trot had carried in the basket.

"Don't you want some, too?" she asked the Glass Cat.

"No," answered the creature.

"I suppose you'll hunt around an' catch a mouse," remarked Cap'n Bill.

"Me? Catch a mouse! Why should I do that?" inquired the Glass Cat.

"Why, then you could eat it," said the sailor-man.

"I beg to inform you," returned the crystal tabby, "that I do not eat mice. Being transparent, so anyone can see through me, I'd look nice, wouldn't I, with a common mouse inside me? But the fact is that I haven't any stomach or other machinery that would permit me to eat things. The careless magician who made me didn't think I'd need to eat, I suppose."

"Don't you ever get hungry or thirsty?" asked Trot.

"Never. I don't complain, you know, at the way

I'm made, for I've never yet seen any living thing as beautiful as I am. I have the handsomest brains in the world. They're pink, and you can see 'em work."

"I wonder," said Trot thoughtfully, as she ate her bread and jam, "if *my* brains whirl around in the same way yours do."

"No; not the same way, surely," returned the Glass Cat; "for, in that case, they'd be as good as *my* brains, except that they're hidden under a thick, boney skull."

"Brains," remarked Cap'n Bill, "is of all kinds and work different ways. But I've noticed that them as thinks that their brains is best is often mistook."

Trot was a little disturbed by sounds from the forest, that night, for many beasts seemed prowling among the trees, but she was confident Cap'n Bill would protect her from harm. And in fact, no beast ventured from the forest to attack them.

At daybreak they were up again, and after a simple breakfast Cap'n Bill said to the Glass Cat:

"Up anchor, Mate, and let's forge ahead. I don't suppose we're far from that Magic Flower, are we?"

"Not far," answered the transparent one, as it led the way into the forest, "but it may take you some time to get to it."

Before long they reached the bank of a river. It was not very wide, at this place, but as they followed the banks in a northerly direction it gradually broadened.

Suddenly the blue-green leaves of the trees changed to a purple hue, and Trot noticed this and said:

"I wonder what made the colors change like that?"

"It's because we have left the Munchkin Country and entered the Gillikin Country," explained the Glass

Cat. " Also it's a sign our journey is nearly ended."

The river made a sudden turn, and after the travelers had passed around the bend, they saw that the stream had now become as broad as a small lake, and in the center of the Lake they beheld a little island, not more than fifty feet in extent, either way. Something glittered in the middle of this tiny island, and the Glass Cat paused on the bank and said:

" There is the gold flower-pot containing the Magic Flower, which is very curious and beautiful. If you can get to the island, your task is ended — except to carry the thing home with you."

Cap'n Bill looked at the broad expanse of water and began to whistle a low, quavering tune. Trot knew that the whistle meant that Cap'n Bill was thinking, and the old sailor didn't look at the island as much as he looked at the trees upon the bank where they stood. Presently he took from the big pocket of his coat an axe-blade, wound in an old cloth to keep the sharp edge from cutting his clothing. Then, with a large pocket knife, he cut a small limb from a tree and whittled it into a handle for his axe.

" Sit down, Trot," he advised the girl, as he worked. " I've got quite a job ahead of me now, for I've got to build us a raft."

The Magic of Oz

"What do we need a raft for, Cap'n?"

"Why, to take us to the island. We can't walk under water, in the river bed, as the Glass Cat did, so we must float atop the water."

"Can you make a raft, Cap'n Bill?"

"O' course, Trot, if you give me time."

The little girl sat down on a log and gazed at the Island of the Magic Flower. Nothing else seemed to grow on the tiny isle. There was no tree, no shrub, no grass, even, as far as she could make out from that distance. But the gold pot glittered in the rays of the sun, and Trot could catch glimpses of glowing colors above it, as the Magic Flower changed from one sort to another.

"When I was here before," remarked the Glass Cat, lazily reclining at the girl's feet, "I saw two Kalidahs on this very bank, where they had come to drink."

"What are Kalidahs?" asked the girl.

"The most powerful and ferocious beasts in all Oz. This forest is their especial home, and so there are few other beasts to be found except monkeys. The monkeys are spry enough to keep out of the way of the fierce Kalidahs, which attack all other animals and often fight among themselves.

The Magic of Oz

"Did they try to fight you when you saw 'em?" asked Trot, getting very much excited.

"Yes. They sprang upon me in an instant; but I lay flat on the ground, so I wouldn't get my legs broken by the great weight of the beasts, and when they tried to bite me I laughed at them and jeered them until they were frantic with rage, for they nearly broke their teeth on my hard glass. So, after a time, they discovered they could not hurt me, and went away. It was great fun."

"I hope they don't come here again to drink,— not while we're here, anyhow," returned the girl, "for I'm not made of glass, nor is Cap'n Bill, and if those bad beasts bit us, we'd get hurt."

Cap'n Bill was cutting from the trees some long stakes, making them sharp at one end and leaving a crotch at the other end. These were to bind the logs of his raft together. He had fashioned several and was just finishing another when the Glass Cat cried: "Look out! There's a Kalidah coming toward us."

Trot jumped up, greatly frightened, and looked at the terrible animal as if fascinated by its fierce eyes, for the Kalidah was looking at her, too, and its look wasn't at all friendly. But Cap'n Bill called to her: "Wade into the river, Trot, up to your knees — an'

stay there!" and she obeyed him at once. The sailor-
man hobbled forward, the stake in one hand and his
axe in the other, and got between the girl and the
beast, which sprang upon him with a growl of defiance.

Cap'n Bill moved pretty slowly, sometimes, but now
he was quick as could be. As the Kalidah sprang
toward him he stuck out his wooden leg and the point
of it struck the beast between its eyes and sent it
rolling upon the ground. Before it could get upon
its feet again the sailor pushed the sharp stake right
through its body and then with the flat side of the
axe he hammered the stake as far into the ground as
it would go. By this means he captured the great
beast and made it harmless, for try as it would, it
could not get away from the stake that held it.

Cap'n Bill knew he could not kill the Kalidah, for
no living thing in Oz can be killed, so he stood back
and watched the beast wriggle and growl and paw
the earth with its sharp claws, and then, satisfied it
could not escape, he told Trot to come out of the water
again and dry her wet shoes and stockings in the
sun.

"Are you sure he can't get away?" she asked.

"I'd bet a cookie on it," said Cap'n Bill, so Trot
came ashore and took off her shoes and stockings and

laid them on the log to dry, while the sailor-man resumed his work on the raft.

The Kalidah, realizing after many struggles that it could not escape, now became quiet, but it said in a harsh, snarling voice:

" I suppose you think you're clever, to pin me to the ground in this manner. But when my friends, the other Kalidahs, come here, they'll tear you to pieces for treating me this way."

" P'raps," remarked Cap'n Bill, coolly, as he chopped at the logs, " an' p'raps not. When are your folks comin' here? "

" I don't know," admitted the Kalidah. " But when they *do* come, you can't escape them."

" If they hold off long enough, I'll have my raft ready," said Cap'n Bill.

" What are you going to do with a raft? " inquired the beast.

" We're goin' over to that island, to get the Magic Flower."

The huge beast looked at him in surprise a moment, and then it began to laugh. The laugh was a good deal like a roar, and it had a cruel and derisive sound, but it was a laugh nevertheless.

" Good! " said the Kalidah. " Good! Very good!

The Magic of Oz

I'm glad you're going to get the Magic Flower. But what will you do with it?"

"We're going to take it to Ozma, as a present on her birthday."

The Kalidah laughed again; then it became sober. "If you get to the land on your raft before my people can catch you," it said, "you will be safe from us. We can swim like ducks, so the girl couldn't have escaped me by getting into the water; but Kalidahs don't go to that island over there."

"Why not?" asked Trot.

The beast was silent.

"Tell us the reason," urged Cap'n Bill.

"Well, it's the Isle of the Magic Flower," answered the Kalidah, "and we don't care much for magic. If you hadn't had a magic leg, instead of a meat one, you couldn't have knocked me over so easily and stuck this wooden pin through me."

"I've been to the Magic Isle," said the Glass Cat, "and I've watched the Magic Flower bloom, and I'm sure it's too pretty to be left in that lonely place where only beasts prowl around it and no one else sees it. So we're going to take it away to the Emerald City."

"I don't care," the beast replied in a surly tone. "We Kalidahs would be just as contented if there

110

wasn't a flower in our forest. What good are the things anyhow?"

"Don't you like pretty things?" asked Trot.

"No."

"You ought to admire my pink brains, anyhow," declared the Glass Cat. "They're beautiful and you can see 'em work."

The beast only growled in reply, and Cap'n Bill, having now cut all his logs to a proper size, began to roll them to the water's edge and fasten them together.

Stuck Fast

CHAPTER 10

The day was nearly gone when, at last, the raft was ready.

"It ain't so very big, said the old sailor, "but I don't weigh much, an' you, Trot, don't weigh half as much as I do, an' the glass pussy don't count."

"But it's safe, isn't it?" inquired the girl.

"Yes; it's good enough to carry us to the island an'

back again, an' that's about all we can expect of it."

Saying this, Cap'n Bill pushed the raft into the water, and when it was afloat, stepped upon it and held out his hand to Trot, who quickly followed him. The Glass Cat boarded the raft last of all.

The sailor had cut a long pole, and had also whittled a flat paddle, and with these he easily propelled the raft across the river. As they approached the island, the Wonderful Flower became more plainly visible, and they quickly decided that the Glass Cat had not praised it too highly. The colors of the flowers that bloomed in quick succession were strikingly bright and beautiful, and the shapes of the blossoms were varied and curious. Indeed, they did not resemble ordinary flowers at all.

So intently did Trot and Cap'n Bill gaze upon the Golden Flower pot that held the Magic Flower that they scarcely noticed the island itself until the raft beached upon its sands. But then the girl exclaimed: "How funny it is, Cap'n Bill, that nothing else grows here excep' the Magic Flower."

Then the sailor glanced at the island and saw that it was all bare ground, without a weed, a stone or a blade of grass. Trot, eager to examine the Flower closer, sprang from the raft and ran up the bank until she reached the Golden Flowerpot. Then she stood beside it motionless and filled with wonder. Cap'n Bill joined her, coming more leisurely, and he, too, stood in silent admiration for a time.

"Ozma will like this," remarked the Glass Cat, sitting down to watch the shifting hues of the flowers. "I'm sure she won't have as fine a birthday present from anyone else."

"Do you 'spose it's very heavy, Cap'n? And can we get it home without breaking it?" asked Trot anxiously.

"Well, I've lifted many bigger things than that," he replied; "but let's see what it weighs."

He tried to take a step forward, but could not lift his meat foot from the ground. His wooden leg seemed free enough, but the other would not budge.

"I seem stuck, Trot," he said, with a perplexed look at his foot. "It ain't mud, an' it ain't glue, but somethin's holdin' me down."

The girl attempted to lift her own feet, to go nearer to her friend, but the ground held them as fast as it held Cap'n Bill's foot. She tried to slide them, or to twist them around, but it was no use; she could not move either foot a hair's breadth.

"This is funny!" she exclaimed. "What do you 'spose has happened to us, Cap'n Bill?"

"I'm tryin' to make out," he answered. "Take off your shoes, Trot. P'raps it's the leather soles that's stuck to the ground."

She leaned down and unlaced her shoes, but found she could not pull her feet out of them. The Glass Cat, which was walking around as naturally as ever, now said:

The Magic of Oz

"Your foot has got roots to it, Cap'n, and I can see the roots going into the ground, where they spread out in all directions. It's the same way with Trot. That's why you can't move. The roots hold you fast."

Cap'n Bill was rather fat and couldn't see his own feet very well, but he squatted down and examined Trot's feet and decided that the Glass Cat was right.

"This is hard luck," he declared, in a voice that showed he was uneasy at the discovery. "We're pris'ners, Trot, on this funny island, an' I'd like to know how we're ever goin' to get loose, so's we can get home again."

"Now I know why the Kalidah laughed at us," said the girl, "and why he said none of the beasts ever came to this island. The horrid creature knew we'd be caught, and wouldn't warn us."

In the meantime, the Kalidah, although pinned fast to the earth by Cap'n Bill's stake, was facing the island, and now the ugly expression which passed over its face when it defied and sneered at Cap'n Bill and Trot, had changed to one of amusement and curiosity. When it saw the adventurers had actually reached the island and were standing beside the Magic Flower, it heaved a breath of satisfaction — a long, deep breath that swelled the deep chest until the

116

beast could feel the stake that held him move a little, as if withdrawing itself from the ground.

"Ah ha!" murmured the Kalidah, "a little more of this will set me free and allow me to escape!"

So he began breathing as hard as he could, puffing out his chest as much as possible with each indrawing breath, and by doing this he managed to raise the stake with each powerful breath, until at last the Kalidah — using the muscles of his four legs as well as his deep breaths — found itself free of the sandy soil. The stake was sticking right through him, however, so he found a rock deeply set in the bank and pressed the sharp point of the stake upon the surface of this rock until he had driven it clear through his body. Then, by getting the stake tangled among some thorny bushes, and wiggling his body, he managed to draw it out altogether.

"There!" he exclaimed, "except for those two holes in me, I'm as good as ever; but I must admit that that old wooden-legged fellow saved both himself and the girl by making me a prisoner."

Now the Kalidahs, although the most disagreeable creatures in the Land of Oz, were nevertheless magical inhabitants of a magical Fairyland, and in their natures a certain amount of good was mingled with

The Magic of Oz

the evil. This one was not very revengeful, and now that his late foes were in danger of perishing, his anger against them faded away.

"Our own Kalidah King," he reflected, "has certain magical powers of his own. Perhaps he knows how to fill up these two holes in my body."

So without paying any more attention to Trot and Cap'n Bill than they were paying to him, he entered the forest and trotted along a secret path that led to the hidden lair of all the Kalidahs.

While the Kalidah was making good its escape Cap'n Bill took his pipe from his pocket and filled it with tobacco and lighted it. Then, as he puffed out the smoke, he tried to think what could be done.

"The Glass Cat seems all right," he said, "an' my wooden leg didn't take roots and grow, either. So it's only flesh that gets caught."

"It's magic that does it, Cap'n!"

"I know, Trot, and that's what sticks me. We're livin' in a magic country, but neither of us knows any magic an' so we can't help ourselves."

"Couldn't the Wizard of Oz help us — or Glinda the Good?" asked the little girl.

"Ah, now we're beginnin' to reason," he answered. "I'd probably thought o' that, myself, in a minute more. By good luck the Glass Cat is free, an' so it can run back to the Emerald City an' tell the Wizard about our fix, an' ask him to come an' help us get loose."

"Will you go?" Trot asked the cat, speaking very earnestly.

"I'm no messenger, to be sent here and there," asserted the curious animal in a sulky tone of voice.

"Well," said Cap'n Bill, "you've got to go home, anyhow, 'cause you don't want to stay here, I take it. And, when you get home, it wouldn't worry you much to tell the Wizard what's happened to us."

"That's true," said the cat, sitting on its haunches and lazily washing its face with one glass paw. "I don't mind telling the Wizard — when I get home."

"Won't you go now?" pleaded Trot. "We don't want to stay here any longer than we can help, and everybody in Oz will be interested in you, and call you a hero, and say nice things about you because you helped your friends out of trouble."

That was the best way to manage the Glass Cat, which was so vain that it loved to be praised.

"I'm going home right away," said the creature, "and I'll tell the Wizard to come and help you."

Saying this, it walked down to the water and dis-

The Magic of Oz

appeared under the surface. Not being able to manage the raft alone, the Glass Cat walked on the bottom
of the river as it had done when it visited the island
before, and soon they saw it appear on the farther
bank and trot into the forest, where it was quickly
lost to sight among the trees.

Then Trot heaved a deep sigh.

"Cap'n," said she, "we're in a bad fix. There's
nothing here to eat, and we can't even lie down to sleep.
Unless the Glass Cat hurries, and the Wizard hurries,
I don't know what's going to become of us!"

The Beasts of the Forest of Gugu

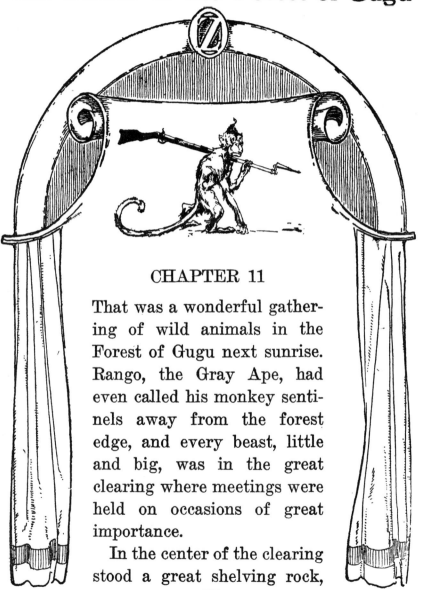

CHAPTER 11

That was a wonderful gather-
ing of wild animals in the
Forest of Gugu next sunrise.
Rango, the Gray Ape, had
even called his monkey senti-
nels away from the forest
edge, and every beast, little
and big, was in the great
clearing where meetings were
held on occasions of great
importance.

In the center of the clearing
stood a great shelving rock,

The Magic of Oz

having a flat, inclined surface, and on this sat the stately Leopard Gugu, who was King of the Forest. On the ground beneath him squatted Bru the Bear, Loo the Unicorn, and Rango the Gray Ape, the King's three Counsellors, and in front of them stood the two strange beasts who had called themselves Li-Mon-Eags, but were really the transformations of Ruggedo the Nome, and Kiki Aru the Hyup.

Then came the beasts — rows and rows and rows of them! The smallest beasts were nearest the King's rock throne; then there were wolves and foxes, lynxes and hyenas, and the like; behind them were gathered the monkey tribes, who were hard to keep in order because they teased the other animals and were full of mischievous tricks. Back of the monkeys were the pumas, jaguars, tigers and lions, and their kind; next the bears, all sizes and colors; after them bisons, wild asses, zebras and unicorns; farther on the rhinoceri and hippopotami, and at the far edge of the forest, close to the trees that shut in the clearing, was a row of thick-skinned elephants, still as statues but with eyes bright and intelligent.

Many other kinds of beasts, too numerous to mention, were there, and some were unlike any beasts we see in the menageries and zoos in our country. Some were from the mountains west of the forest, and some from the plains at the east, and some from the river; but all present acknowledged the leadership of Gugu, who for many years had ruled them wisely and forced all to obey the laws.

When the beasts had taken their places in the clearing and the rising sun was shooting its first bright rays over the treetops, King Gugu rose on his throne. The Leopard's giant form, towering above all the others, caused a sudden hush to fall on the assemblage.

"Brothers," he said in his deep voice, "a stranger has come among us, a beast of curious form who is a great magician and is able to change the shapes of men or beasts at his will. This stranger has come to us, with another of his kind, from out of the sky, to warn us of a danger which threatens us all, and to offer us a way to escape from that danger. He says he is our friend, and he has proved to me and to my counsellors his magic powers. Will you listen to what he has to say to you — to the message he has brought from the sky?"

"Let him speak!" came in a great roar from the great company of assembled beasts.

So Ruggedo the Nome sprang upon the flat rock

The Magic of Oz

beside Gugu the King, and another roar, gentle this time, showed how astonished the beasts were at the sight of his curious form. His lion's face was surrounded by a mane of pure white hair; his eagle's wings were attached to the shoulders of his monkey body and were so long that they nearly touched the ground; he had powerful arms and legs in addition to the wings, and at the end of his long, strong tail was a golden ball. Never had any beast beheld such a curious creature before, and so the very sight of the stranger, who was said to be a great magician, filled all present with awe and wonder.

Kiki stayed down below and, half hidden by the shelf of rock, was scarcely noticed. The boy realized that the old Nome was helpless without his magic power, but he also realized that Ruggedo was the best talker. So he was willing the Nome should take the lead.

"Beasts of the Forest of Gugu," began Ruggedo the Nome, "my comrade and I are your friends. We are magicians, and from our home in the sky we can look down into the Land of Oz and see everything that is going on. Also we can hear what the people below us are saying. That is how we heard Ozma, who rules the Land of Oz, say to her people: 'The beasts in the Forest of Gugu are lazy and are of no use to us. Let us go to their forest and make them all our prisoners. Let us tie them with ropes, and beat them with sticks, until they work for us and become our willing slaves.' And when the people heard Ozma of Oz say this, they were glad and raised a great shout and said: 'We will do it! We will make the beasts of the Forest of Gugu our slaves!'"

The wicked old Nome could say no more, just then, for such a fierce roar of anger rose from the multitude of beasts that his voice was drowned by the clamor. Finally the roar died away, like distant thunder, and Ruggedo the Nome went on with his speech.

"Having heard the Oz people plot against your liberty, we watched to see what they would do, and saw them all begin making ropes — ropes long and short — with which to snare our friends the beasts. You are angry, but we also were angry, for when the Oz people became the enemies of the beasts they also became our enemies; for we, too, are beasts, although we live in the sky. And my comrade and I said: 'We will save our friends and have revenge on the Oz people,' and so we came here to tell you of your danger and of our plan to save you."

The Magic of Oz

"We can save ourselves," cried an old elephant. "We can fight."

"The Oz people are fairies, and you can't fight against magic unless you also have magic," answered the Nome.

"Tell us your plan!" shouted the huge Tiger, and the other beasts echoed his words, crying: "Tell us your plan."

"My plan is simple," replied Ruggedo. "By our magic we will transform all you animals into men and women — like the Oz people — and we will transform all the Oz people into beasts. You can then live in the fine houses of the Land of Oz, and eat the fine food of the Oz people, and wear their fine clothes, and sing and dance and be happy. And the Oz people, having become beasts, will have to live here in the forest and hunt and fight for food, and often go hungry, as you now do, and have no place to sleep but a bed of leaves or a hole in the ground. Having become men and women, you beasts will have all the comforts you desire, and having become beasts, the Oz people will be very miserable. That is our plan, and if you agree to it, we will all march at once into the Land of Oz and quickly conquer our enemies."

When the stranger ceased speaking, a great silence

fell on the assemblage, for the beasts were thinking of what he had said. Finally one of the walrus asked:
"Can you really transform beasts into men, and men into beasts?"

"He can — he can!" cried Loo the Unicorn, prancing up and down in an excited manner. "He transformed *me,* only last evening, and he can transform us all."

The Magic of Oz

Gugu the King now stepped forward.

"You have heard the stranger speak," said he, and now you must answer him. It is for you to decide. Shall we agree to this plan, or not?"

"Yes!" shouted some of the animals.

"No!" shouted others.

And some were yet silent.

Gugu looked around the great circle.

"Take more time to think," he suggested. "Your answer is very important. Up to this time we have had no trouble with the Oz people, but we are proud and free, and never will become slaves. Think carefully, and when you are ready to answer, I will hear you."

Kiki Uses His Magic

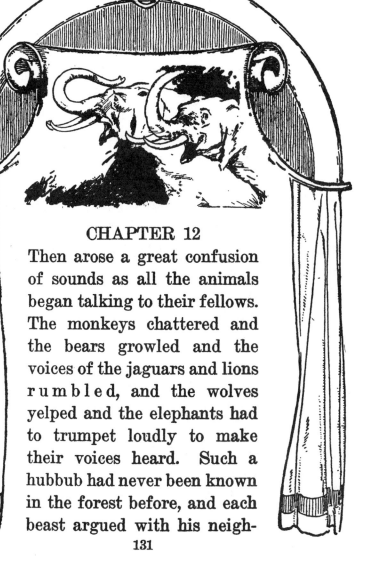

CHAPTER 12

Then arose a great confusion
of sounds as all the animals
began talking to their fellows.
The monkeys chattered and
the bears growled and the
voices of the jaguars and lions
r u m b l e d, and the wolves
yelped and the elephants had
to trumpet loudly to make
their voices heard. Such a
hubbub had never been known
in the forest before, and each
beast argued with his neigh-

bor until it seemed the noise would never cease.

Ruggedo the Nome waved his arms and fluttered his wings to try to make them listen to him again, but the beasts paid no attention. Some wanted to fight the Oz people, some wanted to be transformed, and some wanted to do nothing at all.

The growling and confusion had grown greater than ever when in a flash silence fell on all the beasts present, the arguments were hushed, and all gazed in astonishment at a strange sight.

For into the circle strode a great Lion — bigger and more powerful than any other lion there — and on his back rode a little girl who smiled fearlessly at the multitude of beasts. And behind the lion and the little girl came another beast — a monstrous Tiger, who bore upon his back a funny little man carrying a black bag. Right past the rows of wondering beasts the strange animals walked, advancing until they stood just before the rock throne of Gugu.

Then the little girl and the funny little man dismounted, and the great Lion demanded in a loud voice:

" Who is King in this forest? "

" I am! " answered Gugu, looking steadily at the other. " I am Gugu the Leopard, and I am King of this forest."

"Then I greet Your Majesty with great respect," said the Lion. "Perhaps you have heard of me, Gugu. I am called the 'Cowardly Lion,' and I am King of all Beasts, the world over."

Gugu's eyes flashed angrily.

"Yes," said he, "I have heard of you. You have long claimed to be King of Beasts, but no beast who is a coward can be King over me."

"He isn't a coward, Your Majesty," asserted the little girl, "he's just cowardly, that's all."

Gugu looked at her. All the other beasts were looking at her, too.

"Who are you?" asked the King.

"Me? Oh, I'm just Dorothy," she answered.

"How dare you come here?" demanded the King.

"Why, I'm not afraid to go anywhere, if the Cowardly Lion is with me," she said. "I know him pretty well, and so I can trust him. He's always afraid, when we get into trouble, and that's why he's cowardly; but he's a terrible fighter, and that's why he isn't a coward. He doesn't like to fight, you know, but when he *has* to, there isn't any beast living that can conquer him."

Gugu the King looked at the big, powerful form of the Cowardly Lion, and knew she spoke the truth.

The Magic of Oz

Also the other Lions of the forest now came forward and bowed low before the strange Lion.

"We welcome Your Majesty," said one. "We have known you many years ago, before you went to live at the Emerald City, and we have seen you fight the terrible Kalidahs and conquer them, so we know you are the King of all Beasts."

"It is true," replied the Cowardly Lion; "but I did not come here to rule the beasts of this forest. Gugu is King here, and I believe he is a good King and just and wise. I come, with my friends, to be the guest of Gugu, and I hope we are welcome."

That pleased the great Leopard, who said very quickly:

"Yes; you, at least, are welcome to my forest. But who are these strangers with you."

"Dorothy has introduced herself," replied the Lion, "and you are sure to like her when you know her better. This man is the Wizard of Oz, a friend of mine who can do wonderful tricks of magic. And here is my true and tried friend, the Hungry Tiger, who lives with me in the Emerald City."

"Is he *always* hungry?" asked Loo the Unicorn.

"I am," replied the Tiger, answering the question himself. "I am always hungry for fat babies."

"Can't you find any fat babies in Oz to eat?" inquired Loo, the Unicorn.

"There are plenty of them, of course," said the Tiger, "but unfortunately I have such a tender conscience that it won't allow me to eat babies. So I'm always hungry for 'em and never can eat 'em, because my conscience won't let me."

Now of all the surprised beasts in that clearing, not one was so much surprised at the sudden appearance of these four strangers as Ruggedo the Nome. He was frightened, too, for he recognized them as his most powerful enemies; but he also realized that they could not know he was the former King of the Nomes, because of the beast's form he wore, which disguised him so effectually. So he took courage and resolved that the Wizard and Dorothy should not defeat his plans.

It was hard to tell, just yet, what the vast assemblage of beasts thought of the new arrivals. Some glared angrily at them, but more of them seemed to be curious and wondering. All were interested, however, and they kept very quiet and listened carefully to all that was said.

Kiki Aru, who had remained unnoticed in the shadow of the rock, was at first more alarmed by the coming of the strangers than even Ruggedo was, and the boy told himself that unless he acted quickly and without waiting to ask the advice of the old Nome, their conspiracy was likely to be discovered and all their plans to conquer and rule Oz be defeated. Kiki didn't like the way Ruggedo acted either, for the former King of the Nomes wanted to do everything his own way, and made the boy, who alone possessed the power of transformations, obey his orders as if he were a slave.

Another thing that disturbed Kiki Aru was the fact that a real Wizard had arrived, who was said to possess many magical powers, and this Wizard carried his tools in a black bag, and was the friend of the Oz people, and so would probably try to prevent war between the beasts of the forest and the people of Oz.

All these things passed through the mind of the Hyup boy while the Cowardly Lion and Gugu the King were talking together, and that was why he now began to do several strange things.

He had found a place, near to the point where he stood, where there was a deep hollow in the rock, so he put his face into this hollow and whispered softly, so he would not be heard:

Chapter Twelve

"I want the Wizard of Oz to become a fox — **Pyrzqxgl!**"

The Wizard, who had stood smilingly beside his friends, suddenly felt his form change to that of a fox, and his black bag fell to the ground. Kiki reached out an arm and seized the bag, and the Fox cried as loud as it could:

"Treason! There's a traitor here with magic powers!"

Everyone was startled at this cry, and Dorothy, seeing her old friend's plight, screamed and exclaimed: "Mercy me!"

But the next instant the little girl's form had changed to that of a lamb with fleecy white wool, and Dorothy was too bewildered to do anything but look around her in wonder.

The Cowardly Lion's eyes now flashed fire; he crouched low and lashed the ground with his tail and gazed around to discover who the treacherous magician might be. But Kiki, who had kept his face in the hollow rock, again whispered the magic word, and the great lion disappeared and in his place stood a little boy dressed in Munchkin costume. The little Munchkin boy was as angry as the lion had been, but he was small and helpless.

The Magic of Oz

Ruggedo the Nome saw what was happening and was afraid Kiki would spoil all his plans, so he leaned over the rock and shouted: "Stop, Kiki — stop!"

Kiki would not stop, however. Instead, he transformed the Nome into a goose, to Ruggedo's horror and dismay. But the Hungry Tiger had witnessed all these transformations, and he was watching to see which of those present was to blame for them. When Ruggedo spoke to Kiki, the Hungry Tiger knew that he was the magician, so he made a sudden spring and hurled his great body full upon the form of the Li-Mon-Eag crouching against the rock. Kiki didn't see the Tiger coming because his face was still in the hollow, and the heavy body of the tiger bore him to the earth just as he said "**Pyrzqxgl!**" for the fifth time.

So now the tiger which was crushing him changed to a rabbit, and relieved of its weight, Kiki sprang up and, spreading his eagle's wings, flew into the branches of a tree, where no beast could easily reach him. He was not an instant too quick in doing this, for Gugu the King had crouched on the rock's edge and was about to spring on the boy.

From his tree Kiki transformed Gugu into a fat Gillikin woman, and laughed aloud to see how the

woman pranced with rage, and how astonished all the
beasts were at their King's new shape.

The beasts were frightened, too, fearing they would
share the fate of Gugu, so a stampede began when
Rango the Gray Ape sprang into the forest, and Bru

the Bear and Loo the Unicorn followed as quickly as
they could. The elephants backed into the forest,
and all the other animals, big and little, rushed after
them, scattering through the jungles until the clearing was far behind. The monkeys scrambled into the

trees and swung themselves from limb to limb, to avoid being trampled upon by the bigger beasts, and they were so quick that they distanced all the rest. A panic of fear seemed to have overtaken the forest people and they got as far away from the terrible Magician as they possibly could.

But the transformed ones stayed in the clearing, being so astonished and bewildered by their new shapes that they could only look at one another in a dazed and helpless fashion, although each one was

greatly annoyed at the trick that had been played on him.

"Who are you?" the Munchkin boy asked the Rabbit; and "Who are you?" the Fox asked the Lamb; and "Who are you?" the Rabbit asked the fat Gillikin woman.

"I'm Dorothy," said the woolly Lamb.

"I'm the Wizard," said the Fox.

"I'm the Cowardly Lion," said the Munchkin Boy.

"I'm the Hungry Tiger," said the Rabbit.

"I'm Gugu the King," said the fat Woman.

But when they asked the Goose who he was, Ruggedo the Nome would not tell them.

"I'm just a Goose," he replied, "and what I was before, I cannot remember."

The Loss of the Black Bag

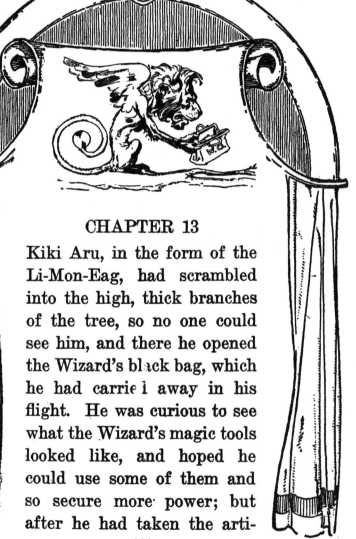

CHAPTER 13

Kiki Aru, in the form of the Li-Mon-Eag, had scrambled into the high, thick branches of the tree, so no one could see him, and there he opened the Wizard's black bag, which he had carried away in his flight. He was curious to see what the Wizard's magic tools looked like, and hoped he could use some of them and so secure more power; but after he had taken the arti-

144

cles, one by one, from the bag, he had to admit they were puzzles to him. For, unless he understood their uses, they were of no value whatever. Kiki Aru, the Hyup boy, was no wizard or magician at all, and could do nothing unusual except to use the Magic Word he had stolen from his father on Mount Munch. So he hung the Wizard's black bag on a branch of the tree and then climbed down to the lower limbs that he might see what the victims of his transformations were doing.

They were all on top of the flat rock, talking together in tones so low that Kiki could not hear what they said.

"This is certainly a misfortune," remarked the Wizard in the Fox's form, "but our transformations are a sort of enchantment which is very easy to break — when you know how and have the tools to do it with. The tools are in my Black Bag; but where is the Bag?"

No one knew that, for none had seen Kiki Aru fly away with it.

"Let's look and see if we can find it," suggested Dorothy the Lamb.

So they left the rock, and all of them searched the clearing high and low without finding the Bag of

145

The Magic of Oz

Magic Tools. The Goose searched as earnestly as the others, for if he could discover it, he meant to hide it where the Wizard could never find it, because if the Wizard changed him back to his proper form, along with the others, he would then be recognized as Ruggedo the Nome, and they would send him out of the Land of Oz and so ruin all his hopes of conquest.

Ruggedo was not really sorry, now that he thought about it, that Kiki had transformed all these Oz folks. The forest beasts, it was true, had been so frightened that they would now never consent to be transformed into men, but Kiki could transform them against their will, and once they were all in human forms, it would not be impossible to induce them to conquer the Oz people.

So all was not lost, thought the old Nome, and the best thing for him to do was to rejoin the Hyup boy who had the secret of the transformations. So, having made sure the Wizard's black bag was not in the clearing, the Goose wandered away through the trees when the others were not looking, and when out of their hearing, he began calling, "Kiki Aru! Kiki Aru! Quack — quack! Kiki Aru!"

The Boy and the Woman, the Fox, the Lamb and

the Rabbit, not being able to find the bag, went back to the rock, all feeling exceedingly strange.

"Where's the Goose?" asked the Wizard.

"He must have run away," replied Dorothy. "I wonder who he was?"

"I think," said Gugu the King, who was the fat Woman, "that the Goose was the stranger who proposed that we make war upon the Oz people. If so, his transformation was merely a trick to deceive us, and he has now gone to join his comrade, that wicked Li-Mon-Eag who obeyed all his commands."

"What shall we do now?" asked Dorothy. "Shall we go back to the Emerald City, as we are, and then visit Glinda the Good and ask her to break the enchantments?"

"I think so," replied the Wizard Fox. "And we can take Gugu the King with us, and have Glinda restore him to his natural shape. But I hate to leave my bag of Magic Tools behind me, for without it I shall lose much of my power as a Wizard. Also, if I go back to the Emerald City in the shape of a Fox, the Oz people will think I'm a poor Wizard and will lose their respect for me."

"Let us make still another search for your tools," suggested the Cowardly Lion, "and then, if we fail

The Magic of Oz

to find the Black Bag anywhere in this forest, we must go back home as we are."

" Why did you come here, anyway? " inquired Gugu.

" We wanted to borrow a dozen monkeys, to use on Ozma's birthday," explained the Wizard. " We were going to make them small, and train them to do tricks, and put them inside Ozma's birthday cake."

" Well," said the Forest King, " you would have to get the consent of Rango the Gray Ape, to do that. He commands all the tribes of monkeys."

" I'm afraid it's too late, now," said Dorothy, regretfully. " It was a splendid plan, but we've got troubles of our own, and I don't like being a lamb at all."

" You're nice and fuzzy," said the Cowardly Lion.

" That's nothing," declared Dorothy. " I've never been 'specially proud of myself, but I'd rather be the way I was born than anything else in the whole world."

❦   ❦   ❦   ❦   ❦   ❦   ❦

The Glass Cat, although it had some disagreeable ways and manners, nevertheless realized that Trot and Cap'n Bill were its friends and so was quite disturbed at the fix it had gotten them into by leading them to the Isle of the Magic Flower. The ruby heart of the Glass Cat was cold and hard, but still it was a heart, and to have a heart of any sort is to have some consideration for others. But the queer transparent creature didn't want Trot and Cap'n Bill to know it was sorry for them, and therefore it moved very slowly until it had crossed the river and was out of sight among the trees of the forest. Then it headed straight toward the Emerald City, and trotted so fast that it was like a crystal streak crossing the valleys and plains. Being glass, the cat was tireless, and with no reason to delay its journey, it reached Ozma's palace in wonderfully quick time.

"Where's the Wizard?" it asked the Pink Kitten, which was curled up in the sunshine on the lowest step of the palace entrance.

"Don't bother me," lazily answered the Pink Kitten, whose name was Eureka.

"I must find the Wizard at once!" said the Glass Cat.

"Then find him," advised Eureka, and went to sleep again.

The Glass Cat darted up the stairway and came upon Toto, Dorothy's little black dog.

"Where's the Wizard?" asked the Cat.

"Gone on a journey with Dorothy," replied Toto.

149

The Magic of Oz

"When did they go, and where have they gone?" demanded the Cat.

"They went yesterday, and I heard them say they would go to the Great Forest in the Munchkin Country."

"Dear me," said the Glass Cat; "that is a long journey."

"But they rode on the Hungry Tiger and the Cowardly Lion," explained Toto, "and the Wizard carried his Black Bag of Magic Tools."

The Glass Cat knew the Great Forest of Gugu well, for it had traveled through this forest many times in its journeys through the Land of Oz. And it reflected that the Forest of Gugu was nearer to the Isle of the Magic Flower than the Emerald City was, and so, if it could manage to find the Wizard, it could lead him across the Gillikin country to where Trot and Cap'n Bill were prisoned. It was a wild country and little traveled, but the Glass Cat knew every path. So very little time need be lost, after all.

Without stopping to ask any more questions the Cat darted out of the palace and away from the Emerald City, taking the most direct route to the Forest of Gugu. Again the creature flashed through the country like a streak of light, and it would surprise you to know how quickly it reached the edge of the Great Forest.

There were no monkey guards among the trees to cry out a warning, and this was so unusual that it astonished the Glass Cat. Going farther into the forest it presently came upon a wolf, which at first

bounded away in terror. But then, seeing it was only a Glass Cat, the Wolf stopped, and the Cat could see it was trembling, as if from a terrible fright.

" What's the matter? " asked the Cat.

" A dreadful Magician has come among us! "

151

The Magic of Oz

exclaimed the Wolf, "and he's changing the forms of all the beasts — quick as a wink — and making them all his slaves."

The Glass Cat smiled and said:

"Why, that's only the Wizard of Oz. He may be having some fun with you forest people, but the Wizard wouldn't hurt a beast for anything."

"I don't mean the Wizard," explained the Wolf. "And if the Wizard of Oz is that funny little man who rode a great Tiger into the clearing, he's been transformed himself by the terrible Magician."

"The Wizard transformed? Why, that's impossible," declared the Glass Cat.

"No; it isn't. I saw him with my own eyes, changed into the form of a Fox, and the girl who was with him was changed to a woolly Lamb."

The Glass Cat was indeed surprised.

"When did that happen?" it asked.

"Just a little while ago in the clearing. All the animals had met there, but they ran away when the Magician began his transformations, and I'm thankful I escaped with my natural shape. But I'm still afraid, and I'm going somewhere to hide."

With this the Wolf ran on, and the Glass Cat, which knew where the big clearing was, went toward it. But now it walked more slowly, and its pink brains rolled and tumbled around at a great rate because it was thinking over the amazing news the Wolf had told it.

When the Glass Cat reached the clearing, it saw a Fox, a Lamb, a Rabbit, a Munchkin boy and a fat Gillikin woman, all wandering around in an aimless sort of way, for they were again searching for the Black Bag of Magic Tools.

The Cat watched them a moment and then it walked slowly into the open space. At once the Lamb ran toward it, crying:

" Oh, Wizard, here's the Glass Cat! "

" Where, Dorothy? " asked the Fox.

" Here! "

The Boy and the Woman and the Rabbit now joined the Fox and the Lamb, and they all stood before the Glass Cat and speaking together, almost like a chorus, asked: " Have you seen the Black Bag? "

" Often," replied the Glass Cat, " but not lately."

" It's lost," said the Fox, " and we must find it."

" Are you the Wizard? " asked the Cat.

" Yes."

" And who are these others? "

" I'm Dorothy," said the Lamb.

" I'm the Cowardly Lion," said the Munchkin boy.

The Magic of Oz

"I'm the Hungry Tiger," said the Rabbit.

"I'm Gugu, King of the Forest," said the fat Woman.

The Glass Cat sat on its hind legs and began to laugh. "My, what a funny lot!" exclaimed the Creature. "Who played this joke on you?"

"It's no joke at all," declared the Wizard. "It was a cruel, wicked transformation, and the Magician that did it has the head of a lion, the body of a monkey, the wings of an eagle and a round ball on the end of his tail."

The Glass Cat laughed again. "That Magician must look funnier than you do," it said. ".Where is he now?"

"Somewhere in the forest," said the Cowardly Lion. "He just jumped into that tall maple tree over there, for he can climb like a monkey and fly like an eagle, and then he disappeared in the forest."

"And there was another Magician, just like him, who was his friend," added Dorothy, "but they probably quarreled, for the wickedest one changed his friend into the form of a Goose."

"What became of the Goose?" asked the Cat, looking around.

"He must have gone away to find his friend," answered Gugu the King. "But a Goose can't travel very fast, so we could easily find him if we wanted to."

"The worst thing of all," said the Wizard, "is that my Black Bag is lost. It disappeaerd when I was transformed. If I could find it I could easily break

these enchantments by means of my magic, and we would resume our own forms again. Will you help us search for the Black Bag, Friend Cat?"

"Of course," replied the Glass Cat. "But I expect the strange Magician carried it away with him. If he's a magician, he knows you need that Bag, and

155

perhaps he's afraid of your magic. So he's probably taken the Bag with him, and you won't see it again unless you find the Magician."

"That sounds reasonable," remarked the Lamb, which was Dorothy. "Those pink brains of yours seem to be working pretty well to-day."

"If the Glass Cat is right," said the Wizard in a solemn voice, "there's more trouble ahead of us. That Magician is dangerous, and if we go near him he may transform us into shapes not as nice as these."

"I don't see how we could be any *worse* off," growled Gugu, who was indignant because he was forced to appear in the form of a fat woman.

"Anyway," said the Cowardly Lion, "our best plan is to find the Magician and try to get the Black Bag from him. We may manage to steal it, or perhaps we can argue him into giving it to us."

"Why not find the Goose, first?" asked Dorothy. "The Goose will be angry at the Magician, and he may be able to help us."

"That isn't a bad idea," returned the Wizard. "Come on, Friends; let's find that Goose. We will separate and search in different directions, and the first to find the Goose must bring him here, where we will all meet again in an hour."

The Wizard Learns the Magic Word

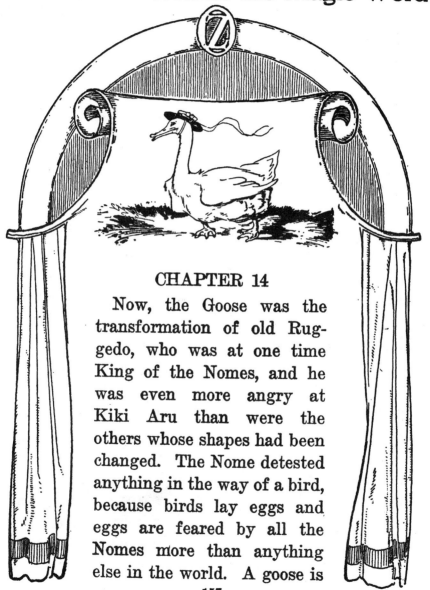

CHAPTER 14

Now, the Goose was the transformation of old Ruggedo, who was at one time King of the Nomes, and he was even more angry at Kiki Aru than were the others whose shapes had been changed. The Nome detested anything in the way of a bird, because birds lay eggs and eggs are feared by all the Nomes more than anything else in the world. A goose is a foolish bird, too, and Ruggedo was dreadfully ashamed of the shape he was forced to wear. And it would make him shudder to reflect that the Goose might lay an egg!

So the Nome was afraid of himself and afraid of everything around him. If an egg touched him he could then be destroyed, and almost any animal he met in the forest might easily conquer him. And that would be the end of old Ruggedo the Nome.

Aside from these fears, however, he was filled with anger against Kiki, whom he had meant to trap by cleverly stealing from him the Magic Word. The boy must have been crazy to spoil everything the way he did, but Ruggedo knew that the arrival of the Wizard had scared Kiki, and he was not sorry the boy had transformed the Wizard and Dorothy and made them helpless. It was his own transformation that annoyed him and made him indignant, so he ran about the forest hunting for Kiki, so that he might get a better shape and coax the boy to follow his plans to conquer the Land of Oz.

Kiki Aru hadn't gone very far away, for he had surprised himself as well as the others by the quick transformations and was puzzled as to what to do next. Ruggedo the Nome was overbearing and tricky, and

Chapter Fourteen

Kiki knew he was not to be depended on; but the Nome could plan and plot, which the Hyup boy was not wise enough to do, and so, when he looked down through the branches of a tree and saw a Goose waddling along below and heard it cry out, "Kiki Aru! Quack — quack! Kiki Aru!" the boy answered in a low voice, "Here I am," and swung himself down to the lowest limb of the tree.

The Goose looked up and saw him.

"You've bungled things in a dreadful way!" exclaimed the Goose. "Why did you do it?"

"Because I wanted to," answered Kiki. "You acted as if I was your slave, and I wanted to show these forest people that I am more powerful than you."

The Goose hissed softly, but Kiki did not hear that.

Old Ruggedo quickly recovered his wits and muttered to himself: "This boy is the goose, although it is I who wear the goose's shape. I will be gentle with him now, and fierce with him when I have him in my power." Then he said aloud to Kiki:

"Well, hereafter I will be content to acknowledge you the master. You bungled things, as I said, but we can still conquer Oz."

"How?" asked the boy.

The Magic of Oz

"First give me back the shape of the Li-Mon-Eag, and then we can talk together more conveniently," suggested the Nome.

"Wait a moment, then," said Kiki, and climbed higher up the tree. There he whispered the Magic Word and the Goose became a Li-Mon-Eag, as he had been before.

"Good!" said the Nome, well pleased, as Kiki joined him by dropping down from the tree. "Now let us find a quiet place where we can talk without being overheard by the beasts."

So the two started away and crossed the forest until they came to a place where the trees were not so tall nor so close together, and among these scattered trees was another clearing, not so large as the first one, where the meeting of the beasts had been held. Standing on the edge of this clearing and looking across it, they saw the trees on the farther side full of monkeys, who were chattering together at a great rate of the sights they had witnessed at the meeting.

The old Nome whispered to Kiki not to enter the clearing or allow the monkeys to see them.

"Why not?" asked the boy, drawing back.

"Because those monkeys are to be our army — the army which will conquer Oz," said the Nome. "Sit

160

down here with me, Kiki, and keep quiet, and I will explain to you my plan."

Now, neither Kiki Aru nor Ruggedo had noticed that a sly Fox had followed them all the way from the tree where the Goose had been transformed to the Li-Mon-Eag. Indeed, this Fox, who was none other than the Wizard of Oz, had witnessed the transformation of the Goose and now decided he would keep watch of the conspirators and see what they would do next.

A Fox can move through a forest very softly, without making any noise, and so the Wizard's enemies did not suspect his presence. But when they sat down by the edge of the clearing, to talk, with their backs toward him, the Wizard did not know whether to risk being seen, by creeping closer to hear what they said, or whether it would be better for him to hide himself until they moved on again.

While he considered this question he discovered near him a great tree which had a hollow trunk, and there was a round hole in this tree, about three feet above the ground. The Wizard Fox decided it would be safer for him to hide inside the hollow tree, so he sprang into the hole and crouched down in the hollow, so that his eyes just came to the edge of the hole by

161

which he had entered, and from here he watched the forms of the two Li-Mon-Eags.

"This is my plan," said the Nome to Kiki, speaking so low that the Wizard could only hear the rumble of his voice. "Since you can transform anything into any form you wish, we will transform these monkeys into an army, and with that army we will conquer the Oz people."

"The monkeys won't make much of an army," objected Kiki.

"We need a great army, but not a numerous one," responded the Nome. "You will transform each monkey into a giant man, dressed in a fine uniform and armed with a sharp sword. There are fifty monkeys over there and fifty giants would make as big an army as we need."

"What will they do with the swords?" asked Kiki. "Nothing can kill the Oz people."

"True," said Ruggedo. "The Oz people cannot be killed, but they can be cut into small pieces, and while every piece will still be alive, we can scatter the pieces around so that they will be quite helpless. Therefore, the Oz people will be afraid of the swords of our army, and we will conquer them with ease."

"That seems like a good idea," replied the boy,

approvingly. " And in such a case, we need not bother with the other beasts of the forest."

" No; you have frightened the beasts, and they would no longer consent to assist us in conquering Oz. But those monkeys are foolish creatures, and once they are transformed to Giants, they will do just as we say and obey our commands. Can you transform them all at once?"

" No, I must take one at a time," said Kiki. " But the fifty transformations can be made in an hour or so. Stay here, Ruggedo, and I will change the first monkey — that one at the left, on the end of the limb — into a Giant with a sword."

" Where are you going?" asked the Nome.

" I must not speak the Magic Word in the presence of another person," declared Kiki, who was determined not to allow his treacherous companion to learn his secret, "so I will go where you cannot hear me."

Ruggedo the Nome was disappointed, but he hoped still to catch the boy unawares and surprise the Magic Word. So he merely nodded his lion head, and Kiki got up and went back into the forest a short distance. Here he spied a hollow tree, and by chance it was the same hollow tree in which the Wizard of Oz, now in the form of a Fox, had hidden himself.

The Magic of Oz

As Kiki ran up to the tree the Fox ducked its head, so that it was out of sight in the dark hollow beneath the hole, and then Kiki put his face into the hole and whispered: "I want that monkey on the branch at the left to become a Giant man fifty feet tall, dressed in a uniform and with a sharp sword—**Pyrzqxgl!**"

Then he ran back to Ruggedo, but the Wizard Fox had heard quite plainly every word that he had said.

The monkey was instantly transformed into the Giant, and the Giant was so big that as he stood on the ground his head was higher than the trees of the forest. The monkeys raised a great chatter but did not seem to understand that the Giant was one of themselves.

"Good!" cried the Nome. "Hurry, Kiki, and transform the others."

So Kiki rushed back to the tree and putting his face to the hollow, whispered:

"I want the next monkey to be just like the first — **Pyrzqxgl!**"

Again the Wizard Fox heard the Magic Word, and just how it was pronounced. But he sat still in the hollow and waited to hear it again, so it would be impressed on his mind and he would not forget it.

Kiki kept running to the edge of the forest and back to the hollow tree again until he had whispered the

Magic Word six times and six monkeys had been changed to six great giants. Then the Wizard decided he would make an experiment and use the Magic Word himself. So, while Kiki was running back to the Nome, the Fox stuck his head out of the

hollow and said softly: "I want that creature who is running to become a hickory-nut — **P y r z q x g l !**"

Instantly the Li-Mon-Eag form of Kiki Aru the Hyup disappeared and a small hickory-nut rolled upon the ground a moment and then lay still.

165

The Magic of Oz

The Wizard was delighted, and leaped from the hollow just as Ruggedo looked around to see what had become of Kiki. The Nome saw the Fox but no Kiki, so he hastily rose to his feet. The Wizard did not know how powerful the queer beast might be, so he resolved to take no chances.

"I want this creature to become a walnut — **Pyrzqxgl!**" he said aloud. But he did not pronounce the Magic Word in quite the right way, and Ruggedo's form did not change. But the Nome knew at once that "**Pyrzqxgl!**" was the Magic Word, so he rushed at the Fox and cried:

"I want you to become a Goose — **Pyrzqxgl!**"

But the Nome did not pronounce the word aright, either, having never heard it spoken but once before, and then with a wrong accent. So the Fox was not transformed, but it had to run away to escape being caught by the angry Nome.

Ruggedo now began pronouncing the Magic Word in every way he could think of, hoping to hit the right one, and the Fox, hiding in a bush, was somewhat troubled by the fear that he might succeed. However, the Wizard, who was used to magic arts, remained calm and soon remembered exactly how Kiki Aru had pronounced the word. So he repeated the sentence

he had before uttered and Ruggedo the Nome became
an ordinary walnut.

The Wizard now crept out from the bush and said:
" I want my own form again — **P y r z q x g l !** "

Instantly he was the Wizard of Oz, and after picking
up the hickory-nut and the walnut, and carefully placing them in his pocket, he ran back to the big clearing.

Dorothy the Lamb uttered a bleat of delight when
she saw her old friend restored to his natural shape.

167

The Magic of Oz

The others were all there, not having found the Goose. The fat Gillikin woman, the Munchkin boy, the Rabbit and the Glass Cat crowded around the Wizard and asked what had happened.

Before he explained anything of his adventure, he transformed them all — except, of course, the Glass Cat — into their natural shapes, and when their joy permitted them to quiet somewhat, he told how he had by chance surprised the Magician's secret and been able to change the two Li-Mon-Eags into shapes that could not speak, and therefore would be unable to help themselves. And the little Wizard showed his astonished friends the hickory-nut and the walnut to prove that he had spoken the truth.

"But — see here!" — exclaimed Dorothy, "What has become of those Giant Soldiers who used to be monkeys?"

"I forgot all about them!" admitted the Wizard; "but I suppose they are still standing there in the forest."

The Lonesome Duck

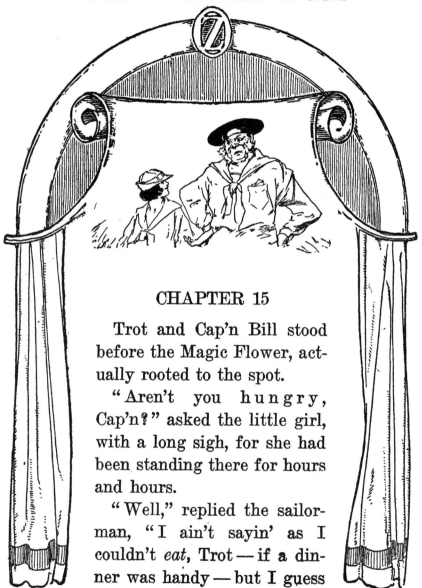

CHAPTER 15

Trot and Cap'n Bill stood before the Magic Flower, actually rooted to the spot.

"Aren't you hungry, Cap'n?" asked the little girl, with a long sigh, for she had been standing there for hours and hours.

"Well," replied the sailorman, "I ain't sayin' as I couldn't *eat*, Trot — if a dinner was handy — but I guess old folks don't get as hungry as young folks do."

"I'm not sure 'bout that, Cap'n Bill," she said thoughtfully. "Age *might* make a diff'rence, but seems to me *size* would make a bigger diff'rence. Seeing you're twice as big as me, you ought to be twice as hungry."

"I hope I am," he rejoined, "for I can stand it a while longer. I do hope the Glass Cat will hurry, and I hope the Wizard won't waste time a-comin' to us."

Trot sighed again and watched the wonderful Magic Flower, because there was nothing else to do. Just now a lovely group of pink peonies budded and bloomed, but soon they faded away, and a mass of deep blue lilies took their place. Then some yellow chrysanthemums blossomed on the plant, and when they had opened all their petals and reached perfection, they gave way to a lot of white floral balls spotted with crimson — a flower Trot had never seen before.

"But I get awful tired watchin' flowers an' flowers an' flowers," she said impatiently.

"They're mighty pretty," observed Cap'n Bill.

"I know; and if a person could come and look at the Magic Flower just when she felt like it, it would be a fine thing, but to *have to* stand and watch it, whether you want to or not, isn't so much fun. I wish, Cap'n

Bill, the thing would grow fruit for a while instead of flowers."

Scarcely had she spoken when the white balls with crimson spots faded away and a lot of beautiful ripe peaches took their place. With a cry of mingled surprise and delight Trot reached out and plucked a peach from the bush and began to eat it, finding it delicious. Cap'n Bill was somewhat dazed at the girl's wish being granted so quickly, so before he could pick a peach they had faded away and bananas took their place. " Grab one, Cap'n!" exclaimed Trot, and even while eating the peach she seized a banana with her other hand and tore it from the bush.

The old sailor was still bewildered. He put out a hand indeed, but he was too late, for now the bananas disappeared and lemons took their place.

" Pshaw!" cried Trot. " You can't eat those things; but watch out, Cap'n, for something else."

" Cocoanuts next appeared, but Cap'n Bill shook his head.

" Ca'n't crack 'em," he remarked, " 'cause we haven't anything handy to smash 'em with."

" Well, take one, anyhow," advised Trot; but the cocoanuts were gone now, and a deep, purple, pear-shaped fruit which was unknown to them took their place. Again Cap'n Bill hesitated, and Trot said to him:

" You ought to have captured a peach and a banana, as I did. If you're not careful, Cap'n, you'll miss all your chances. Here, I'll divide my banana with you."

Even as she spoke, the Magic Plant was covered with big red apples, growing on every branch, and Cap'n Bill hesitated no longer. He grabbed with both hands and picked two apples, while Trot had only time to secure one before they were gone.

" It's curious," remarked the sailor, munching his apple, " how these fruits keep good when you've picked 'em, but dis'pear inter thin air if they're left on the bush."

" The whole thing is curious," declared the girl, " and it couldn't exist in any country but this, where magic is so common. Those are limes. Don't pick 'em, for they'd pucker up your mouth and — Ooo! here come plums! " and she tucked her apple in her apron pocket and captured three plums — each one almost as big as an egg — before they disappeared. Cap'n Bill got some too, but both were too hungry to fast any longer, so they began eating their apples and plums and let the magic bush bear all sorts of fruits, one after another. The Cap'n stopped once to pick a fine canta-

loupe, which he held under his arm, and Trot, having finished her plums, got a handful of cherries and an orange; but when almost every sort of fruit had appeared on the bush, the crop ceased and only flowers, as before, bloomed upon it.

"I wonder why it changed back," mused Trot, who was not worried because she had enough fruit to satisfy her hunger.

"Well, you only wished it would bear fruit 'for a while,'" said the sailor, "and it did. P'raps if you'd said 'forever,' Trot, it would have always been fruit."

"But why should *my* wish be obeyed?" asked the girl. "I'm not a fairy or a wizard or any kind of a magic-maker."

"I guess," replied Cap'n Bill, "that this little island is a magic island, and any folks on it can tell the bush what to produce, an' it'll produce it."

"Do you think I could wish for anything else, Cap'n, and get it?" she inquired anxiously.

"What are you thinkin' of, Trot?"

"I'm thinking of wishing that these roots on our feet would disappear, and let us free."

"Try it, Trot."

So she tried it, and the wish had no effect whatever.

"Try it yourself, Cap'n," she suggested.

Then Cap'n Bill made the wish to be free, with no better result.

"No," said he, "it's no use; the wishes only affect the Magic Plant; but I'm glad we can make it bear fruit, 'cause now we know we won't starve before the Wizard gets to us."

"But I'm gett'n' tired standing here so long," complained the girl. "If I could only lift one foot, and rest it, I'd feel better."

"Same with me, Trot. I've noticed that if you've got to do a thing, and can't help yourself, it gets to be a hardship mighty quick."

"Folks that can raise their feet don't appreciate what a blessing it is," said Trot thoughtfully. "I never knew before what fun it is to raise one foot, an' then another, any time you feel like it."

"There's lots o' things folks don't 'preciate," replied the sailor-man. "If somethin' would 'most stop your breath, you'd think breathin' easy was the finest thing in life. When a person's well, he don't realize how jolly it is, but when he gets sick he 'members the time he was well, an' wishes that time would come back. Most folks forget to thank God for givin' 'em two good legs, till they lose one o' 'em, like I did; and then it's too late, 'cept to praise God for leavin' one."

The Magic of Oz

"Your wooden leg ain't so bad, Cap'n," she remarked, looking at it critically. "Anyhow, it don't take root on a Magic Island, like our meat legs do."

"I ain't complainin'," said Cap'n Bill. "What's that swimmin' towards us, Trot?" he added, looking over the Magic Flower and across the water.

The girl looked, too, and then she replied.

"It's a bird of some sort. It's like a duck, only I never saw a duck have so many colors."

The bird swam swiftly and gracefully toward the Magic Isle, and as it drew nearer its gorgeously colored plumage astonished them. The feathers were of many hues of glistening greens and blues and purples, and it had a yellow head with a red plume, and pink, white and violet in its tail. When it reached the Isle, it came ashore and approached them, waddling slowly and turning its head first to one side and then to the other, so as to see the girl and the sailor better.

"You're strangers," said the bird, coming to a halt near them, "and you've been caught by the Magic Isle and made prisoners."

"Yes," returned Trot, with a sigh; "we're rooted. But I hope we won't grow."

"You'll grow small," said the Bird. "You'll keep

176

growing smaller every day, until bye and bye there'll be nothing left of you. That's the usual way, on this Magic Isle."

"How do you know about it, and who are you, anyhow?" asked Cap'n Bill.

"I'm the Lonesome Duck," replied the bird. "I suppose you've heard of me?"

"No," said Trot, "I can't say I have. What makes you lonesome?"

"Why, I haven't any family or any relations," returned the Duck.

The Magic of Oz

"Haven't you any friends?"

"Not a friend. And I've nothing to do. I've lived a long time, and I've got to live forever, because I belong in the Land of Oz, where no living thing dies. Think of existing year after year, with no friends, no family, and nothing to do! Can you wonder I'm lonesome?"

"Why don't you make a few friends, and find something to do?" inquired Cap'n Bill.

"I can't make friends because everyone I meet — bird, beast or person — is disagreeable to me. In a few minutes I shall be unable to bear your society longer, and then I'll go away and leave you," said the Lonesome Duck. "And, as for doing anything, there's no use in it. All I meet are doing something, so I have decided it's common and uninteresting and I prefer to remain lonesome."

"Don't you have to hunt for your food?" asked Trot.

"No. In my diamond palace, a little way up the river, food is magically supplied me; but I seldom eat, because it is só common."

"You must be a Magician Duck," remarked Cap'n Bill.

"Why so?"

Chapter Fifteen

"Well, ordinary ducks don't have diamond palaces an' magic food, like you do."

"True; and that's another reason why I'm lonesome. You must remember I'm the only Duck in the Land of Oz, and I'm not like any other duck in the outside world."

"Seems to me you *like* bein' lonesome," observed Cap'n Bill.

"I can't say I like it, exactly," replied the Duck, "but since it seems to be my fate, I'm rather proud of it."

"How do you s'pose a single, solitary Duck happened to be in the Land of Oz?" asked Trot, wonderingly.

"I used to know the reason, many years ago, but I've quite forgotten it," declared the Duck. "The reason for a thing is never so important as the thing itself, so there's no use remembering anything but the fact that I'm lonesome."

"I guess you'd be happier if you tried to do something," asserted Trot. "If you can't do anything for yourself, you can do things for others, and then you'd get lots of friends and stop being lonesome."

"Now you're getting disagreeable," said the Lonesome Duck, "and I shall have to go and leave you."

The Magic of Oz

"Can't you help us any," pleaded the girl. "If there's anything magic about you, you might get us out of this scrape."

"I haven't any magic strong enough to get you off the Magic Isle," replied the Lonesome Duck. "What magic I possess is very simple, but I find it enough for my own needs."

"If we could only sit down a while, we could stand it better," said Trot, "but we have nothing to sit on."

"Then you will have to stand it," said the Lonesome Duck.

"P'raps you've enough magic to give us a couple of stools," suggested Cap'n Bill.

"A duck isn't supposed to know what stools are," was the reply.

"But you're diff'rent from all other ducks."

"That is true." The strange creature seemed to reflect for a moment, looking at them sharply from its round black eyes. Then it said: "Sometimes, when the sun is hot, I grow a toadstool to shelter me from its rays. Perhaps you could sit on toadstools."

"Well, if they were strong enough, they'd do." answered Cap'n Bill.

"Then, before I go I'll give you a couple," said the Lonesome Duck, and began waddling about in a small

180

circle. It went around the circle to the right three times, and then it went around to the left three times. Then it hopped backward three times and forward three times.

"What are you doing?" asked Trot.

"Don't interrupt. This is an incantation," replied the Lonesome Duck, but now it began making a succession of soft noises that sounded like quacks and seemed to mean nothing at all. And it kept up these sounds so long that Trot finally exclaimed:

"Can't you hurry up and finish that 'cantation? If it takes all summer to make a couple of toadstools, you're not much of a magician."

"I told you not to interrupt," said the Lonesome Duck, sternly. "If you get *too* disagreeable, you'll drive me away before I finish this incantation."

Trot kept quiet, after the rebuke, and the Duck resumed the quacky muttering. Cap'n Bill chuckled a little to himself and remarked to Trot in a whisper: "For a bird that ain't got anything to do, this Lonesome Duck is makin' consider'ble fuss. An' I ain't sure, after all, as toadstools would be worth sittin' on."

Even as he spoke, the sailor-man felt something touch him from behind and, turning his head, he found a big toadstool in just the right place and of just the

181

right size to sit upon. There was one behind Trot, too, and with a cry of pleasure the little girl sank back upon it and found it a very comfortable seat — solid, yet almost like a cushion. Even Cap'n Bill's weight did not break his toadstool down, and when both were seated, they found that the Lonesome Duck had waddled away and was now at the water's edge.

"Thank you, ever so much!" cried Trot, and the sailor called out: "Much obliged!"

But the Lonesome Duck paid no attention. Without even looking in their direction again, the gaudy fowl entered the water and swam gracefully away.

The Glass Cat Finds the Black Bag

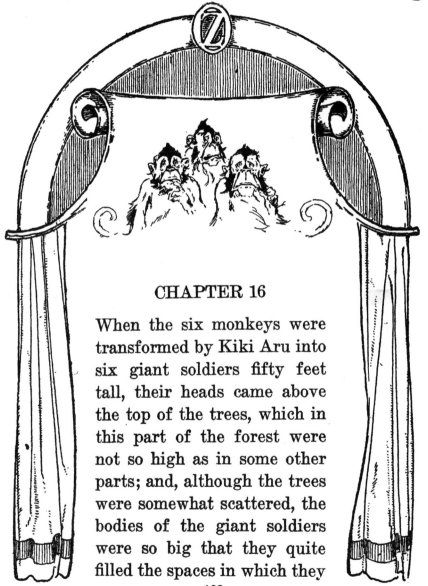

CHAPTER 16

When the six monkeys were
transformed by Kiki Aru into
six giant soldiers fifty feet
tall, their heads came above
the top of the trees, which in
this part of the forest were
not so high as in some other
parts; and, although the trees
were somewhat scattered, the
bodies of the giant soldiers
were so big that they quite
filled the spaces in which they

The Magic of Oz

stood and the branches pressed them on every side.

Of course, Kiki was foolish to have made his soldiers so big, for now they could not get out of the forest. Indeed, they could not stir a step, but were imprisoned by the trees. Even had they been in the little clearing they could not have made their way out of it, but they were a little beyond the clearing. At first, the other monkeys who had not been enchanted were afraid of the soldiers, and hastily quitted the place; but soon finding that the great men stood stock still, although grunting indignantly at their transformation, the band of monkeys returned to the spot and looked at them curiously, not guessing that they were really monkeys and their own friends.

The soldiers couldn't see them, their heads being above the trees; they could not even raise their arms or draw their sharp swords, so closely were they held by the leafy branches. So the monkeys, finding the giants helpless, began climbing up their bodies, and presently all the band were perched on the shoulders of the giants and peering into their faces.

"I'm Ebu, your father," cried one soldier to a monkey who had perched upon his left ear, "but some cruel person has enchanted me."

184

Chapter Sixteen

"I'm your Uncle Peeker," said another soldier to another monkey.

So, very soon all the monkeys knew the truth and were sorry for their friends and relations and angry at the person — whoever it was — who had transformed them. There was a great chattering among the tree-tops, and the noise attracted other monkeys, so that the clearing and all the trees around were full of them.

Rango the Gray Ape, who was the Chief of all the monkey tribes of the forest, heard the uproar and came to see what was wrong with his people. And Rango, being wiser and more experienced, at once knew that the strange magician who looked like a mixed-up beast was responsible for the transformations. He realized that the six giant soldiers were helpless prisoners, because of their size, and knew he was powerless to release them. So, although he feared to meet the terrible magician, he hurried away to the great clearing to tell Gugu the King what had happened and to try to find the Wizard of Oz and get him to save his six enchanted subjects.

Rango darted into the Great Clearing just as the Wizard had restored all the enchanted ones around him to their proper shapes, and the Gray Ape was

glad to hear that the wicked magician-beast had been conquered.

"But now, O mighty Wizard, you must come with me to where six of my people are transformed into six great giant men," he said, "for if they are allowed to remain there, their happiness and their future lives will be ruined."

The Wizard did not reply at once, for he was thinking this a good opportunity to win Rango's consent to his taking some monkeys to the Emerald City for Ozma's birthday cake.

"It is a great thing you ask of me, O Rango the Gray Ape," said he, "for the bigger the giants are the more powerful their enchantment, and the more difficult it will be to restore them to their natural forms. However, I will think it over."

Then the Wizard went to another part of the clearing and sat on a log and appeared to be in deep thought.

The Glass Cat had been greatly interested in the Gray Ape's story and was curious to see what the giant soldiers looked like. Hearing that their heads extended above the tree-tops, the Glass Cat decided that if it climbed the tall avocado tree that stood at the side of the clearing, it might be able to see the giants' heads. So, without mentioning her errand, the crystal creature went to the tree and, by sticking her sharp glass claws in the bark, easily climbed the tree to its very top and, looking over the forest, saw the six giant heads, although they were now a long way off. It was, indeed, a remarkable sight, for the huge heads had immense soldier caps on them, with red and yellow plumes and looked very fierce and terrible, although the monkey hearts of the giants were at that moment filled with fear.

Having satisfied her curiosity, the Glass Cat began to climb down from the tree more slowly. Suddenly she discerned the Wizard's black bag hanging to a limb of the tree. She grasped the black bag in her glass teeth, and although it was rather heavy for so small an animal, managed to get it free and to carry it safely down to the ground. Then she looked around for the Wizard and seeing him seated upon the stump she hid the black bag among some leaves and then went over to where the Wizard sat.

"I forgot to tell you," said the Glass Cat, "that Trot and Cap'n Bill are in trouble, and I came here to hunt you up and get you to go and rescue them."

"Good gracious, Cat! Why didn't you tell me before?" exclaimed the Wizard.

189

The Magic of Oz

"For the reason that I found so much excitement here that I forgot Trot and Cap'n Bill."

"What's wrong with them?" asked the Wizard.

Then the Glass Cat explained how they had gone to get the Magic Flower for Ozma's birthday gift and had been trapped by the magic of the queer island. The Wizard was really alarmed, but he shook his head and said sadly:

"I'm afraid I can't help my dear friends, because I've lost my black bag."

"If I find it, will you go to them?" asked the creature.

"Of course," replied the Wizard. "But I do not think that a Glass Cat with nothing but pink brains can succeed when all the rest of us have failed."

"Don't you admire my pink brains?" demanded the Cat.

"They're pretty," admitted the Wizard, "but they're not regular brains, you know, and so we don't expect them to amount to much."

"But if I find your black bag — and find it inside of five minutes — will you admit my pink brains are better than your common human brains?"

"Well, I'll admit they're better *hunters*," said the Wizard, reluctantly, "but you can't do it. We've searched everywhere, and the black bag isn't to be found."

"That shows how much you know!" retorted the Glass Cat, scornfully. "Watch my brains a minute, and see them whirl around."

The Wizard watched, for he was anxious to regain his black bag, and the pink brains really did whirl around in a remarkable manner.

"Now, come with me," commanded the Glass Cat, and led the Wizard straight to the spot where it had

The Magic of Oz

covered the bag with leaves. "According to my brains," said the creature, "your black bag ought to be here."

Then it scratched at the leaves and uncovered the bag, which the Wizard promptly seized with a cry of delight. Now that he had regained his Magic Tools, he felt confident he could rescue Trot and Cap'n Bill.

Rango the Gray Ape was getting impatient. He now approached the Wizard and said:

"Well, what do you intend to do about those poor enchanted monkeys?"

"I'll make a bargain with you, Rango," replied the little man. "If you will let me take a dozen of your monkeys to the Emerald City, and keep them until after Ozma's birthday, I'll break the enchantment of the six Giant Soldiers and return them to their natural forms."

But the Gray Ape shook his head.

"I can't do it," he declared. "The monkeys would be very lonesome and unhappy in the Emerald City and your people would tease them and throw stones at them, which would cause them to fight and bite."

"The people won't see them till Ozma's birthday dinner," promised the Wizard. "I'll make them very small — about four inches high, and I'll keep them in a pretty cage in my own room, where they will be safe from harm. I'll feed them the nicest kind of food, train them to do some clever tricks, and on Ozma's birthday I'll hide the twelve little monkeys inside a cake. When Ozma cuts the cake the monkeys will jump out on to the table and do their tricks. The next day I will bring them back to the forest and make them big as ever, and they'll have some exciting stories to tell their friends. What do you say, Rango?"

"I say no!" answered the Gray Ape. "I won't have my monkeys enchanted and made to do tricks for the Oz people."

"Very well," said the Wizard calmly; "then I'll go. Come, Dorothy," he called to the little girl, "let's start on our journey."

"Aren't you going to save those six monkeys who are giant soldiers?" asked Rango, anxiously.

"Why should I?" returned the Wizard. "If you will not do me the favor I ask, you cannot expect me to favor you."

"Wait a minute," said the Gray Ape. "I've changed my mind. If you will treat the twelve monkeys nicely and bring them safely back to the forest, I'll let you take them."

The Magic of Oz

"Thank you," replied the Wizard, cheerfully. "We'll go at once and save those giant soldiers."

So all the party left the clearing and proceeded to the place where the giants still stood among the trees. Hundreds of monkeys, apes, baboons and orang-outangs had gathered round, and their wild chatter could be heard a mile away. But the Gray Ape soon hushed the babel of sounds, and the Wizard lost no time in breaking the enchantments. First one and then another giant soldier disappeared and became an ordinary monkey again, and the six were shortly returned to their friends in their proper forms.

This action made the Wizard very popular with the great army of monkeys, and when the Gray Ape announced that the Wizard wanted to borrow twelve monkeys to take to the Emerald City for a couple of weeks, and asked for volunteers, nearly a hundred offered to go, so great was their confidence in the little man who had saved their comrades.

The Wizard selected a dozen that seemed intelligent and good-tempered, and then he opened his black bag and took out a queerly shaped dish that was silver on the outside and gold on the inside. Into this dish he poured a powder and set fire to it. It made a thick smoke that quite enveloped the twelve monkeys, as well as the form of the Wizard, but when the smoke cleared away the dish had been changed to a golden cage with silver bars, and the twelve monkeys had become about three inches high and

were all seated comfortably inside the cage.

The thousands of hairy animals who had witnessed this act of magic were much astonished and applauded the Wizard by barking aloud and shaking the limbs

The Magic of Oz

of the trees in which they sat. Dorothy said: "That was a fine trick, Wizard!" and the Gray Ape remarked: "You are certainly the most wonderful magician in all the Land of Oz!"

"Oh, no," modestly replied the little man. "Glinda's magic is better than mine, but mine seems good enough to use on ordinary occasions. And now, Rango, we will say good-bye, and I promise to return your monkeys as happy and safe as they are now."

The Wizard rode on the back of the Hungry Tiger and carried the cage of monkeys very carefully, so as not to joggle them. Dorothy rode on the back of the Cowardly Lion, and the Glass Cat trotted, as before, to show them the way.

Gugu the King crouched upon a log and watched them go, but as he bade them farewell, the enormous leopard said:

"I know now that you are the friends of beasts and that the forest people may trust you. Whenever the Wizard of Oz and Princess Dorothy enter the Forest of Gugu hereafter, they will be as welcome and as safe with us as ever they are in the Emerald City."

A Remarkable Journey

CHAPTER 17

"You see," explained the Glass Cat, "that Magic Isle where Trot and Cap'n Bill are stuck is also in this Gillikin country — over at the east side of it, and it's no farther to go across-lots from here than it is from here to the Emerald City. So we'll save time by cutting across the mountains."

"Are you sure you know the way?" asked Dorothy.

The Magic of Oz

"I know all the Land of Oz better than any other living creature knows it," asserted the Glass Cat.

"Go ahead, then, and guide us," said the Wizard. "We've left our poor friends helpless too long already, and the sooner we rescue them the happier they'll be."

"Are you sure you can get 'em out of their fix?" the little girl inquired.

"I've no doubt of it," the Wizard assured her. "But I can't tell what sort of magic I must use until I get to the place and discover just how they are enchanted."

"I've heard of that Magic Isle where the Wonderful Flower grows," remarked the Cowardly Lion. "Long ago, when I used to live in the forests, the beasts told stories about the Isle and how the Magic Flower was placed there to entrap strangers — men or beasts."

"Is the Flower really wonderful?" questioned Dorothy.

"I have heard it is the most beautiful plant in the world," answered the Lion. "I have never seen it myself, but friendly beasts have told me that they have stood on the shore of the river and looked across at the plant in the gold flowerpot and seen hundreds of flowers, of all sorts and sizes, blossom upon it in quick succession. It is said that if one picks the

198

flowers while they are in bloom they will remain perfect for a long time, but if they are not picked they soon disappear and are replaced by other flowers. That, in my opinion, makes the magic plant the most wonderful in existence."

"But these are only stories," said the girl. "Has any of your friends ever picked a flower from the wonderful plant?"

"No," admitted the Cowardly Lion, "for if any living thing ventures upon the Magic Isle, where the golden flowerpot stands, that man or beast takes root in the soil and cannot get away again."

"What happens to them, then?" asked Dorothy.

"They grow smaller, hour by hour and day by day, and finally disappear entirely."

"Then," said the girl anxiously, "we must hurry up, or Cap'n Bill an' Trot will get too small to be comf'table."

They were proceeding at a rapid pace during this conversation, for the Hungry Tiger and the Cowardly Lion were obliged to move swiftly in order to keep pace with the Glass Cat. After leaving the Forest of Gugu they crossed a mountain range, and then a broad plain, after which they reached another forest, much smaller than that where Gugu ruled.

The Magic of Oz

"The Magic Isle is in this forest," said the Glass Cat, "but the river is at the other side of the forest. There is no path through the trees, but if we keep going east, we will find the river, and then it will be easy to find the Magic Isle."

"Have you ever traveled this way before?" inquired the Wizard.

"Not exactly," admitted the Cat, "but I know we shall reach the river if we go east through the forest."

"Lead on, then," said the Wizard.

"The Glass Cat started away, and at first it was easy to pass between the trees; but before long the underbrush and vines became thick and tangled, and after pushing their way through these obstacles for a time, our travelers came to a place where even the Glass Cat could not push through.

"We'd better go back and find a path," suggested the Hunger Tiger.

"I'm s'prised at you," said Dorothy, eyeing the Glass Cat severely.

"I'm surprised, myself," replied the Cat. "But it's a long way around the forest to where the river enters it, and I thought we could save time by going straight through."

"No one can blame you," said the Wizard, "and I

think, instead of turning back, I can make a path that will allow us to proceed."

He opened his black bag and after searching among his magic tools drew out a small axe, made of some metal so highly polished that it glittered brightly even in the dark forest. The Wizard laid the little axe on the ground and said in a commanding voice:

"Chop, Little Axe, chop clean and true;
A path for our feet you must quickly hew.
Chop till this tangle of jungle is passed;
Chop to the east, Little Axe — chop fast!"

Then the little axe began to move and flashed its bright blade right and left, clearing a way through vine and brush and scattering the tangled barrier so quickly that the Lion and the Tiger, carrying Dorothy and the Wizard. and the cage of monkeys on their backs, were able to stride through the forest at a fast walk. The brush seemed to melt away before them and the little axe chopped so fast that their eyes only saw a twinkling of the blade. Then, suddenly, the forest was open again, and the little axe, having obeyed its orders, lay still upon the ground.

The Wizard picked up the magic axe and after carefully wiping it with his silk handkerchief put it away in his black bag. Then they went on and in a short time reached the river.

"Let me see," said the Glass Cat, looking up and down the stream, "I think we are below the Magic Isle; so we must go up the stream until we come to it."

So up the stream they traveled, walking comfortably on the river bank, and after a while the water broadened and a sharp bend appeared in the river, hiding all below from their view. They walked briskly along, however, and had nearly reached the bend when a voice cried warningly: "Look out!"

The travelers halted abruptly and the Wizard said: "Look out for what?"

"You almost stepped on my Diamond Palace," replied the voice, and a duck with gorgeously colored feathers appeared before them. "Beasts and men are terribly clumsy," continued the Duck in an irritated tone, "and you've no business on this side of the river, anyway. What are you doing here?"

"We've come to rescue some friends of ours who are stuck fast on the Magic Isle in this river," explained Dorothy.

"I know 'em," said the Duck. "I've been to see 'em, and they're stuck fast, all right. You may as well go back home, for no power can save them."

Chapter Seventeen

"This is the Wonderful Wizard of Oz," said Dorothy, pointing to the little man.

"Well, I'm the Lonesome Duck," was the reply, as the fowl strutted up and down to show its feathers to best advantage. "I'm the great Forest Magician,

as any beast can tell you, but even I have no power to destroy the dreadful charm of the Magic Isle."

"Are you lonesome because you're a magician?" inquired Dorothy.

"No; I'm lonesome because I have no family and

no friends. But I like to be lonesome, so please don't offer to be friendly with me. Go away, and try not to step on my Diamond Palace."

"Where is it?" asked the girl.

"Behind this bush."

Dorothy hopped off the lion's back and ran around the bush to see the Diamond Palace of the Lonesome Duck, although the gaudy fowl protested in a series of low quacks. The girl found, indeed, a glistening dome formed of clearest diamonds, neatly cemented together, with a doorway at the side just big enough to admit the duck.

"Where did you find so many diamonds?" asked Dorothy, wonderingly.

"I know a place in the mountains where they are thick as pebbles," said the Lonesome Duck, "and I brought them here in my bill, one by one and put them in the river and let the water run over them until they were brightly polished. Then I built this palace, and I'm positive it's the only Diamond Palace in all the world."

"It's the only one I know of," said the little girl; "but if you live in it all alone, I don't see why it's any better than a wooden palace, or one of bricks or cobble-stones."

"You're not supposed to understand that," retorted the Lonesome Duck. "But I might tell you, as a matter of education, that a home of any sort should be beautiful to those who live in it, and should not

be intended to please strangers. The Diamond Palace is my home, and I like it. So I don't care a quack whether *you* like it or not."

"Oh, but I do!" exclaimed Dorothy. "It's lovely on the outside, but—" Then she stopped speaking,

The Magic of Oz

for the Lonesome Duck had entered his palace through the little door without even saying good-bye. So Dorothy returned to her friends and they resumed their journey.

"Do you think, Wizard, the Duck was right in saying no magic can rescue Trot and Cap'n Bill?" asked the girl in a worried tone of voice.

"No, I don't think the Lonesome Duck was right in saying that," answered the Wizard, gravely, "but it is possible that their enchantment will be harder to overcome than I expected. I'll do my best, of course, and no one can do more than his best."

That didn't entirely relieve Dorothy's anxiety, but she said nothing more, and soon, on turning the bend in the river, they came in sight of the Magic Isle.

"There they are!" exclaimed Dorothy eagerly.

"Yes, I see them," replied the Wizard, nodding. "They are sitting on two big toadstools."

"That's queer," remarked the Glass Cat. "There were no toadstools there when I left them."

"What a lovely flower!" cried Dorothy in rapture, as her gaze fell on the Magic Plant.

"Never mind the Flower, just now," advised the Wizard. "The most important thing is to rescue our friends."

By this time they had arrived at a place just opposite the Magic Isle, and now both Trot and Cap'n Bill saw the arrival of their friends and called to them for help.

"How are you?" shouted the Wizard, putting his

hands to his mouth so they could hear him better across the water.

"We're in hard luck," shouted Cap'n Bill, in reply. "We're anchored here and can't move till you find a way to cut the hawser."

The Magic of Oz

"What does he mean by that?" asked Dorothy.

"We can't move our feet a bit!" called Trot, speaking as loud as she could.

"Why not?" inquired Dorothy.

"They've got roots on 'em," explained Trot.

It was hard to talk from so great a distance, so the Wizard said to the Glass Cat:

"Go to the island and tell our friends to be patient, for we have come to save them. It may take a little time to release them, for the Magic of the Isle is new to me and I shall have to experiment. But tell them I'll hurry as fast as I can."

So the Glass Cat walked across the river under the water to tell Trot and Cap'n Bill not to worry, and the Wizard at once opened his black bag and began to make his preparations.

The Magic of the Wizard

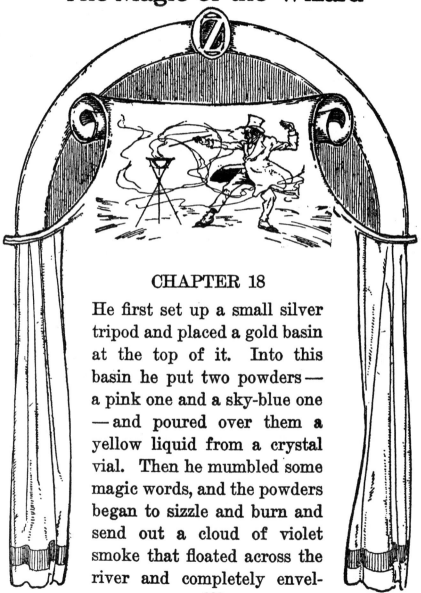

CHAPTER 18

He first set up a small silver tripod and placed a gold basin at the top of it. Into this basin he put two powders — a pink one and a sky-blue one — and poured over them a yellow liquid from a crystal vial. Then he mumbled some magic words, and the powders began to sizzle and burn and send out a cloud of violet smoke that floated across the river and completely envel-

The Magic of Oz

oped both Trot and Cap'n Bill, as well as the toad-stools on which they sat, and even the **Magic Plant** in the gold flowerpot. Then, after the smoke had disappeared into air, the Wizard called out to the prisoners:

"Are you free?"

Both Trot and Cap'n Bill tried to move their feet and failed.

"No!" they shouted in answer.

The Wizard rubbed his bald head thoughtfully and then took some other magic tools from the bag.

First he placed a little black ball in a silver pistol and shot it toward the Magic Isle. The ball exploded just over the head of Trot and scattered a thousand sparks over the little girl.

"Oh!" said the Wizard, "I guess that will set her free."

But Trot's feet were still rooted in the ground of the Magic Isle, and the disappointed Wizard had to try something else.

For almost an hour he worked hard, using almost every magic tool in his black bag, and still Cap'n Bill and Trot were not rescued.

"Dear me!" exclaimed Dorothy, "I'm 'fraid we'll have to go to Glinda, after all."

Chapter Eighteen

That made the little Wizard blush, for it shamed him to think that his magic was not equal to that of the Magic Isle.

"I won't give up yet, Dorothy," he said, "for I know a lot of wizardry that I haven't yet tried. I don't know what magician enchanted this little island, or what his powers were, but I *do* know that I can break any enchantment known to the ordinary witches and magicians that used to inhabit the Land of Oz. It's like unlocking a door; all you need is to find the right key."

"But 'spose you haven't the right key with you," suggested Dorothy; "what then?"

"Then we'll have to make the key," he answered.

The Glass Cat now came back to their side of the river, walking under the water, and said to the Wizard: "They're getting frightened over there on the island because they're both growing smaller every minute. Just now, when I left them, both Trot and Cap'n Bill were only about half their natural sizes,"

"I think," said the Wizard reflectively, "that I'd better go to the shore of the island, where I can talk to them and work to better advantage. How did Trot and Cap'n Bill get to the island?"

"On a raft," answered the Glass Cat. "It's over there now on the beach."

"I suppose you're not strong enough to bring the raft to this side, are you?"

"No; I couldn't move it an inch," said the Cat.

"I'll try to get it for you," volunteered the Cowardly Lion. "I'm dreadfully scared for fear the Magic Isle will capture me, too; but I'll try to get the raft and bring it to this side for you."

"Thank you, my friend," said the Wizard.

So the Lion plunged into the river and swam with powerful strokes across to where the raft was beached upon the island. Placing one paw on the raft, he turned and struck out with his other three legs and so strong was the great beast that he managed to drag the raft from off the beach and propel it slowly to where the Wizard stood on the river bank.

"Good!" exclaimed the little man, well pleased.

"May I go across with you?" asked Dorothy.

The Wizard hesitated.

"If you'll take care not to leave the raft or step foot on the island, you'll be quite safe," he decided. So the Wizard told the Hungry Tiger and the Cowardly Lion to guard the cage of monkeys until he returned, and then he and Dorothy got upon the raft.

The Magic of Oz

The paddle which Cap'n Bill had made was still there, so the little Wizard paddled the clumsy raft across the water and ran it upon the beach of the Magic Isle as close to the place where Cap'n Bill and Trot were rooted as he could.

Dorothy was shocked to see how small the prisoners had become, and Trot said to her friends: "If you can't save us soon, there'll be nothing left of us."

"Be patient, my dear," counselled the Wizard, and took the little axe from his black bag.

"What are you going to do with that?" asked Cap'n Bill.

"It's a magic axe," replied the Wizard, "and when I tell it to chop, it will chop those roots from your feet and you can run to the raft before they grow again."

"Don't!" shouted the sailor in alarm. "Don't do it! Those roots are all flesh roots, and our bodies are feeding 'em while they're growing into the ground."

"To cut off the roots," said Trot, "would be like cutting off our fingers and toes."

The Wizard put the little axe back in the black bag and took out a pair of silver pincers.

"Grow — grow — grow!" he said to the pincers, and at once they grew and extended until they reached from the raft to the prisoners.

"What are you going to do now?" demanded Cap'n Bill, fearfully eyeing the pincers.

"This magic tool will pull you up, roots and all, and land you on this raft," declared the Wizard.

"Don't do it!" pleaded the sailor, with a shudder. "It would hurt us awfully."

"It would be just like pulling teeth to pull us up by the roots," explained Trot.

"Grow small!" said the Wizard to the pincers, and at once they became small and he threw them into the black bag.

The Magic of Oz

"I guess, friends, it's all up with us, this time," remarked Cap'n Bill, with a dismal sigh.

"Please tell Ozma, Dorothy," said Trot, "that we got into trouble trying to get her a nice birthday present. Then she'll forgive us. The Magic Flower is lovely and wonderful, but it's just a lure to catch folks on this dreadful island and then destroy them. You'll have a nice birthday party, without us, I'm sure; and I hope, Dorothy, that none of you in the Emerald City will forget me — or dear ol' Cap'n Bill."

Dorothy and the Bumble Bees

CHAPTER 19

Dorothy was g r e a t l y distressed and had hard work to keep the tears from her eyes.

"Is that all you can do, Wizard?" she asked the little man.

"It's all I can think of just now," he replied sadly. "But I intend to keep on thinking as long — as long — well, as long as thinking will do any good."

They were all silent for a

The Magic of Oz

time, Dorothy and the Wizard sitting thoughtfully on the raft, and Trot and Cap'n Bill sitting thoughtfully on the toadstools and growing gradually smaller and smaller in size.

Suddenly Dorothy said: " Wizard, I've thought of something!"

"What have you thought of?" he asked, looking at the little girl with interest.

" Can you remember the 'Magic Word that transforms people?" she asked.

" Of course," said he.

" Then you can transform Trot and Cap'n Bill into birds or Bumblebees, and they can fly away to the other shore. When they're there, you can transform 'em into their reg'lar shapes again!"

" Can you do that, Wizard?" asked Cap'n Bill, eagerly.

" I think so."

" Roots an' all?" inquired Trot.

" Why, the roots are now a part of you, and if you were transformed to a bumble-bee the whole of you would be transformed, of course, and you'd be free of this awful island."

" All right; do it!" cried the sailor man.

So the Wizard said slowly and distinctly:

218

"I want Trot and Cap'n Bill to become bumble-bees — **Pyrzqxgl!**"

Fortunately, he pronounced the Magic Word in the right way, and instantly Trot and Cap'n Bill vanished from view, and up from the places where they had been flew two bumble-bees.

"Hooray!" shouted Dorothy in delight; "they're saved!"

"I guess they are," agreed the Wizard, equally delighted.

The bees hovered over the raft an instant and then flew across the river to where the Lion and the Tiger waited. The Wizard picked up the paddle and paddled the raft across as fast as he could. When it reached the river bank, both Dorothy and the Wizard leaped ashore and the little man asked excitedly:

"Where are the bees?"

"The bees?" inquired the Lion, who was half asleep and did not know what had happened on the Magic Isle.

"Yes; there were two of them."

"Two bees?" said the Hungry Tiger, yawning. "Why, I ate one of them and the Cowardly Lion ate the other."

"Goodness gracious!" cried Dorothy horrified.

The Magic of Oz

"It was little enough for our lunch," remarked the Tiger, "but the bees were the only things we could find."

"How dreadful!" wailed Dorothy, wringing her hands in despair. "You've eaten Trot and Cap'n Bill."

But just then she heard a buzzing overhead and two bees alighted on her shoulder.

"Here we are," said a small voice in her ear. "I'm Trot, Dorothy."

"And I'm Cap'n Bill," said the other bee.

Dorothy almost fainted, with relief, and the Wizard, who was close by and had heard the tiny voices, gave a laugh and said:

"You are not the only two bees in the forest, it seems, but I advise you to keep away from the Lion and the Tiger until you regain your proper forms."

"Do it now, Wizard!" advised Dorothy. "They're so small that you never can tell what might happen to 'em."

So the Wizard gave the command and pronounced the Magic Word, and in the instant Trot and Cap'n Bill stood beside them as natural as before they had met their fearful adventure. For they were no longer small in size, because the Wizard had transformed them from bumble-bees into the shapes and sizes that nature had formerly given them. The ugly roots on their feet had disappeared with the transformation. While Dorothy was hugging Trot, and Trot was

softly crying because she was so happy, the Wizard shook hands with Cap'n Bill and congratulated him on his escape. The old sailor-man was so pleased that he also shook the Lion's paw and took off his hat and bowed politely to the cage of monkeys.

The Magic of Oz

Then Cap'n Bill did a curious thing. He went to a big tree and, taking out his knife, cut away a big, broad piece of thick bark. Then he sat down on the ground and after taking a roll of stout cord from his pocket — which seemed to be full of all sorts of things — he proceeded to bind the flat piece of bark to the bottom of his good foot, over the leather sole.

"What's that for?" inquired the Wizard.

"I hate to be stumped," replied the sailor-man; "so I'm goin' back to that island."

"And get enchanted again?" exclaimed Trot, with evident disapproval.

"No; this time I'll dodge the magic of the island. I noticed that my wooden leg didn't get stuck, or take root, an' neither did the glass feet of the Glass Cat. It's only a thing that's made of meat — like man an' beasts — that the magic can hold an' root to the ground. Our shoes are leather, an' leather comes from a beast's hide. Our stockin's are wool, an' wool comes from a sheep's back. So, when we walked on the Magic Isle, our feet took root there an' held us fast. But not my wooden leg. So now I'll put a wooden bottom on my other foot an' the magic can't stop me."

"But why do you wish to go back to the island?" asked Dorothy.

"Didn't you see the Magic Flower in the gold flower-pot?" returned Cap'n Bill.

"Of course I saw it, and it's lovely and wonderful."

"Well, Trot an' I set out to get that magic plant for a present to Ozma on her birthday, and I mean to get it an' take it back with us to the Emerald City."

"That would be fine," cried Trot eagerly, "if you think you can do it, and it would be safe to try!"

"I'm pretty sure it is safe, the way I've fixed my foot," said the sailor, "an' if I *should* happen to get caught, I s'pose the Wizard could save me again."

"I suppose I could," agreed the Wizard. "Anyhow, if you wish to try it, Cap'n Bill, go ahead and we'll stand by and watch what happens."

So the sailor-man got upon the raft again and paddled over to the Magic Isle, landing as close to the golden flower-pot as he could. They watched him walk across the land, put both arms around the flower-pot and lift it easily from its place. Then he carried it to the raft and set it down very gently. The removal did not seem to affect the Magic Flower in any way, for it was growing daffodils when Cap'n Bill picked it up and on the way to the raft it grew tulips and gladioli. During the time the sailor was paddling across the river to where his friends awaited him, seven dif-

The Magic of Oz

ferent varieties of flowers bloomed in succession on the plant.

"I guess the Magician who put it on the island never thought that any one would carry it off," said Dorothy.

"He figured that only men would want the plant, and any man who went upon the island to get it would be caught by the enchantment," added the Wizard.

"After this," remarked Trot, "no one will care to go on the island, so it won't be a trap any more."

"There," exclaimed Cap'n Bill, setting down the Magic Plant in triumph upon the river bank, "if Ozma gets a better birthday present than that, I'd like to know what it can be!"

"It'll s'prise her, all right," declared Dorothy, standing in awed wonder before the gorgeous blossoms and watching them change from yellow roses to violets.

"It'll s'prise ev'rybody in the Em'rald City," Trot asserted in glee, "and it'll be Ozma's present from Cap'n Bill and me."

"I think *I* ought to have a little credit," objected the Glass Cat. "I discovered the thing, and led you to it, and brought the Wizard here to save you when you got caught."

"That's true," admitted Trot, "and I'll tell Ozma the whole story, so she'll know how good you've been."

The Monkeys Have Trouble

CHAPTER 20

"Now," said the Wizard, "we must start for home. But how are we going to carry that big gold flowerpot? Cap'n Bill can't lug it all the way, that's certain."

"No," acknowledged the sailor-man; "it's pretty heavy. I could carry it for a little while, but I'd have to stop to rest every few minutes."

"Couldn't we put it on your back?" Dorothy asked the

Cowardly Lion, with a good-natured yawn.

"I don't object to carrying it, if you can fasten it on," answered the Lion.

"If it falls off," said Trot, "it might get smashed an' be ruined."

"I'll fix it," promised Cap'n Bill. "I'll make a flat board out of one of these tree trunks, an' tie the board on the lion's back, an' set the flowerpot on the board." He set to work at once to do this, but as he only had his big knife for a tool his progress was slow.

So the Wizard took from his black bag a tiny saw that shone like silver and said to it:

"Saw, little Saw, come show your power;
Make us a board for the Magic Flower."

And at once the Little Saw began to move and it sawed the log so fast that those who watched it work were astonished. It seemed to understand, too, just what the board was to be used for, for when it was completed it was flat on top and hollowed beneath in such a manner that it exactly fitted the Lion's back.

"That beats whittlin'!" exclaimed Cap'n Bill, admiringly. "You don't happen to have *two* o' them saws; do you, Wizard?"

"No," replied the Wizard, wiping the Magic Saw

carefully with his silk handkerchief and putting it back in the black bag. "It's the only saw of its kind in the world; and if there were more like it, it wouldn't be so wonderful."

They now tied the board on the Lion's back, flat side up, and Cap'n Bill carefully placed the Magic Flower on the board.

"For fear o' accidents," he said, "I'll walk beside the lion and hold onto the flowerpot."

Trot and Dorothy could both ride on the back of the Hungry Tiger, and between them they carried the cage of monkeys. But this arrangement left the Wizard, as well as the sailor, to make the journey on foot, and so the procession moved slowly and the Glass Cat grumbled because it would take so long to get to the Emerald City.

The Cat was sour-tempered and grumpy, at first, but before they had journeyed far, the crystal creature had discovered a fine amusement. The long tails of the monkeys were constantly sticking through the bars of their cage, and when they did, the Glass Cat would slyly seize the tails in her paws and pull them. That made the monkeys scream, and their screams pleased the Glass Cat immensely. Trot and Dorothy tried to stop this naughty amusement, but when they were not looking the Cat would pull the tails again, and the creature was so sly and quick that the monkeys could seldom escape. They scolded the Cat angrily and shook the bars of their cage, but they could not

get out and the Cat only laughed at them.

After the party had left the forest and were on the plains of the Munchkin Country, it grew dark, and they were obliged to make camp for the night, choosing a pretty place beside a brook. By means of his

The Magic of Oz

magic the Wizard created three tents, pitched in a row on the grass and nicely fitted with all that was needful for the comfort of his comrades. The middle tent was for Dorothy and Trot, and had in it two cosy white beds and two chairs. Another tent, also with beds and chairs, was for the Wizard and Cap'n Bill, while the third tent was for the Hungry Tiger, the Cowardly Lion, the cage of Monkeys and the Glass Cat. Outside the tents the Wizard made a fire and placed over it a magic kettle from which he presently drew all sorts of nice things for their supper, smoking hot.

After they had eaten and talked together for a while under the twinkling stars, they all went to bed and the people were soon asleep. The Lion and the Tiger had almost fallen asleep, too, when they were roused by the screams of the monkeys, for the Glass Cat was pulling their tails again. Annoyed by the uproar, the Hungry Tiger cried: "Stop that racket!" and getting sight of the Glass Cat, he raised his big paw and struck at the creature. The cat was quick enough to dodge the blow, but the claws of the Hungry Tiger scraped the monkeys' cage and bent two of the bars.

Then the Tiger lay down again to sleep, but the monkeys soon discovered that the bending of the bars would allow them to squeeze through. They did not leave the cage, however, but after whispering together they let their tails stick out and all remained quiet. Presently the Glass Cat stole near the cage again and gave a yank to one of the tails. Instantly the monkeys leaped through the bars, one after another, and although they were so small the entire dozen of them surrounded the Glass Cat and clung to

her claws and tail and ears and made her a prisoner. Then they forced her out of the tent and down to the banks of the stream. The monkeys had noticed that these banks were covered with thick, slimy mud of a dark blue color, and when they had taken the Cat to the stream, they smeared this mud all over the glass body of the cat, filling the creature's ears and eyes with it, so that she could neither see nor hear. She was no longer transparent and so thick was the mud upon her that no one could see her pink brains or her ruby heart.

In this condition they led the pussy back to the tent and then got inside their cage again.

By morning the mud had dried hard on the Glass Cat and it was a dull blue color throughout. Dorothy and Trot were horrified, but the Wizard shook his head and said it served the Glass Cat right for teasing the monkeys.

Cap'n Bill, with his strong hands, soon bent the golden wires of the monkeys' cage into the proper position and then he asked the Wizard if he should wash the Glass Cat in the water of the brook.

"Not just yet," answered the Wizard. "The Cat deserves to be punished, so I think I'll leave that blue mud — which is as bad as paint — upon her body until she gets to the Emerald City. The silly creature is so vain that she will be greatly shamed when the Oz people see her in this condition, and perhaps she'll take the lesson to heart and leave the monkeys alone hereafter."

However, the Glass Cat could not see or hear, and to avoid carrying her on the journey the Wizard picked the mud out of her eyes and ears and Dorothy dampened her handkerchief and washed both the eyes and ears clean.

As soon as she could speak the Glass Cat asked indignantly: "Aren't you going to punish those monkeys for playing such a trick on me?"

"No," answered the Wizard. "You played a trick on them by pulling their tails, so this is only tit-for-tat, and I'm glad the monkeys had their revenge."

He wouldn't allow the Glass Cat to go near the water, to wash herself, but made her follow them when they resumed their journey toward the Emerald City.

"This is only part of your punishment," said the Wizard, severely. "Ozma will laugh at you, when we get to her palace, and so will the Scarecrow, and the Tin Woodman, and Tik-Tok, and the Shaggy Man, and Button-Bright, and the Patchwork Girl, and —"

"And the Pink Kitten," added Dorothy.

That suggestion hurt the Glass Cat more than anything else. The Pink Kitten always quarreled with the Glass Cat and insisted that flesh was superior to glass, while the Glass Cat would jeer at the Pink Kitten, because it had no pink brains. But the pink brains were all daubed with blue mud, just now, and if the Pink Kitten should see the Glass Cat in such a condition, it would be dreadfully humiliating.

For several hours the Glass Cat walked along very meekly, but toward noon it seized an opportunity when no one was looking and darted away through the long grass. It remembered that there was a tiny lake of pure water near by, and to this lake the Cat sped as fast as it could go.

The others never missed her until they stopped for lunch, and then it was too late to hunt for her.

"I s'pect she's gone somewhere to clean herself," said Dorothy.

"Never mind," replied the Wizard. "Perhaps this glass creature has been punished enough, and we must not forget she saved both Trot and Cap'n Bill."

"After first leading 'em onto an enchanted island," added Dorothy. "But I think, as you do, that the Glass Cat is punished enough, and p'raps she won't try to pull the monkeys' tails again."

The Glass Cat did not rejoin the party of travelers. She was still resentful, and they moved too slowly to suit her, besides. When they arrived at the Royal Palace, one of the first things they saw was the Glass Cat curled up on a bench as bright and clean and transparent as ever. But she pretended not to notice them, and they passed her by without remark.

The College of Athletic Arts

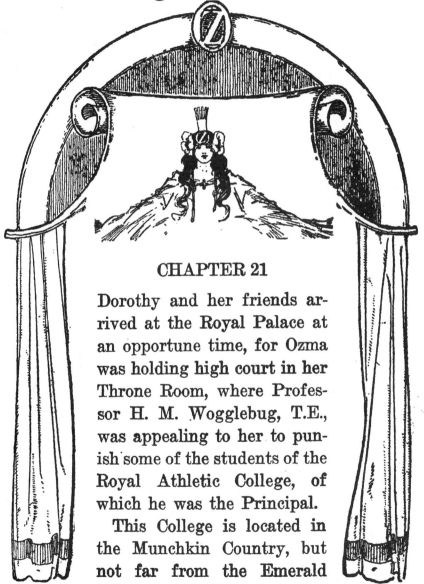

CHAPTER 21

Dorothy and her friends arrived at the Royal Palace at an opportune time, for Ozma was holding high court in her Throne Room, where Professor H. M. Wogglebug, T.E., was appealing to her to punish some of the students of the Royal Athletic College, of which he was the Principal.

This College is located in the Munchkin Country, but not far from the Emerald

The Magic of Oz

City. To enable the students to devote their entire time to athletic exercises, such as boating, foot-ball, and the like, Professor Wogglebug had invented an assortment of Tablets of Learning. One of these tablets, eaten by a scholar after breakfast, would instantly enable him to understand arithmetic or algebra or any other branch of mathematics. Another tablet eaten after lunch gave a student a complete knowledge of geography. Another tablet made it possible for the eater to spell the most difficult words, and still another enabled him to write a beautiful hand. There were tablets for history, mechanics, home cooking and agriculture, and it mattered not whether a boy or a girl was stupid or bright, for the tablets taught them everything in the twinkling of an eye.

This method, which is patented in the Land of Oz by Professor Wogglebug, saves paper and books, as well as the tedious hours devoted to study in some of our less favored schools, and it also allows the students to devote all their time to racing, base-ball, tennis and other manly and womanly sports, which are greatly interfered with by study in those Temples of Learning where Tablets of Learning are unknown.

But it so happened that Professor Wogglebug (who had invented so much that he had acquired the habit)

carelessly invented a Square-Meal Tablet, which was no bigger than your little finger-nail but contained, in condensed form, the equal of a bowl of soup, a portion of fried fish, a roast, a salad and a dessert, all of which gave the same nourishment as a square meal.

The Professor was so proud of these Square-Meal Tablets that he began to feed them to the students at his college, instead of other food, but the boys and girls objected because they wanted food that they could enjoy the taste of. It was no fun at all to swallow a tablet, with a glass of water, and call it a dinner; so they refused to eat the Square-Meal Tablets. Professor Wogglebug insisted, and the result was that the Senior Class seized the learned Professor one day and threw him into the river — clothes and all. Everyone knows that a wogglebug cannot swim, and so the inventor of the wonderful Square-Meal Tablets lay helpless on the bottom of the river for three days before a fisherman caught one of his legs on a fishhook and dragged him out upon the bank.

The learned Professor was naturally indignant at such treatment, and so he brought the entire senior class to the Emerald City and appealed to Ozma of Oz to punish them for their rebellion.

The Magic of Oz

I do not suppose the girl Ruler was very severe with the rebellious boys and girls, because she had herself refused to eat the Square-Meal Tablets in place of food, but while she was listening to the interesting case in her Throne Room, Cap'n Bill managed to carry the golden flower-pot containing the Magic Flower up to Trot's room without it being seen by anyone except Jellia Jamb, Ozma's chief Maid of Honor, and Jellia promised not to tell.

Also the Wizard was able to carry the cage of monkeys up to one of the top towers of the palace, where he had a room of his own, to which no one came unless invited. So Trot and Dorothy and Cap'n Bill and the Wizard were all delighted at the successful end of their adventure. The Cowardly Lion and the Hungry Tiger went to the marble stables behind the Royal Palace, where they lived while at home, and they too kept the secret, even refusing to tell the Wooden Sawhorse, and Hank the Mule, and the Yellow Hen, and the Pink Kitten where they had been.

Trot watered the Magic Flower every day and allowed no one in her room to see the beautiful blossoms except her friends, Betsy Bobbin and Dorothy. The wonderful plant did not seem to lose any of its magic by being removed from its island,

and Trot was sure that Ozma would prize it as one of her most delightful treasures.

Up in his tower the little Wizard of Oz began training his twelve tiny monkeys, and the little creatures were so intelligent that they learned every trick the Wizard tried to teach them. The Wizard treated them with great kindness and gentleness and gave them the food that monkeys love best, so they promised to do their best on the great occasion of Ozma's birthday.

Ozma's Birthday Party

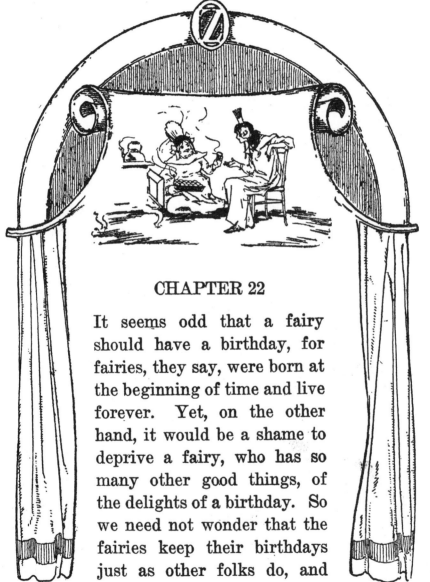

CHAPTER 22

It seems odd that a fairy
should have a birthday, for
fairies, they say, were born at
the beginning of time and live
forever. Yet, on the other
hand, it would be a shame to
deprive a fairy, who has so
many other good things, of
the delights of a birthday. So
we need not wonder that the
fairies keep their birthdays
just as other folks do, and

consider them occasions for feasting and rejoicing.

Ozma, the beautiful girl Ruler of the Fairyland of Oz, was a real fairy, and so sweet and gentle in caring for her people that she was greatly beloved by them all. She lived in the most magnificent palace in the most magnificent city in the world, but that did not prevent her from being the friend of the most humble person in her dominions. She would mount her wooden Sawhorse, and ride out to a farm house and sit in the kitchen to talk with the good wife of the farmer while she did her family baking; or she would play with the children and give them rides on her famous wooden steed; or she would stop in a forest to speak to a charcoal burner and ask if he was happy or desired anything to make him more content; or she would teach young girls how to sew and plan pretty dresses, or enter the shops where the jewelers and craftsmen were busy and watch them at their work, giving to each and all a cheering word or sunny smile.

And then Ozma would sit in her jeweled throne, with her chosen courtiers all about her, and listen patiently to any complaint brought to her by her subjects, striving to accord equal justice to all. Knowing she was fair in her decisions, the Oz people never murmured at her judgments, but agreed, if Ozma

The Magic of Oz

decided against them, she was right and they wrong.

When Dorothy and Trot and Betsy Bobbin and Ozma were together, one would think they were all about of an age, and the fairy Ruler no older and no more " grown up " than the other three. She would laugh and romp with them in regular girlish fashion, yet there was an air of quiet dignity about Ozma, even in her merriest moods, that, in a manner, distinguished her from the others. The three girls loved her devotedly, but they were never able to quite forget that Ozma was the Royal Ruler of the wonderful fairyland of Oz, and by birth belonged to a powerful race.

Ozma's palace stood in the center of a delightful and extensive garden, where splendid trees and flowering shrubs and statuary and fountains abounded. One could walk for hours in this fascinating park and see something interesting at every step. In one place was an aquarium, where strange and beautiful fish swam; at another spot all the birds of the air gathered daily to a great feast which Ozma's servants provided for them, and were so fearless of harm that they would alight upon one's shoulders and eat from one's hand. There was also the Fountain of the Water of Oblivion, but it was dangerous to drink of this water, because it made one forget everything

The Magic of Oz

he had ever before known, even to his own name, and therefore Ozma had placed a sign of warning upon the fountain. But there were also fountains that were delightfully perfumed, and fountains of delicious nectar, cool and richly flavored, where all were welcome to refresh themselves.

Around the palace grounds was a great wall, thickly encrusted with glittering emeralds, but the gates stood open and no one was forbidden entrance. On holidays the people of the Emerald City often took their children to see the wonders of Ozma's gardens, and even entered the Royal Palace, if they felt so inclined, for they knew that they and their Ruler were friends, and that Ozma delighted to give them pleasure.

When all this is considered, you will not be surprised that the people throughout the Land of Oz, as well as Ozma's most intimate friends and her royal courtiers, were eager to celebrate her birthday, and made preparations for the festival weeks in advance. All the brass bands practiced their nicest tunes, for they were to march in the numerous processions to be made in the Winkie Country, the Gillikin Country, the Munchkin Country and the Quadling Country, as well as in the Emerald City. Not all the people could go to congratulate their Ruler, but all could celebrate her birthday, in one way or another, however far distant from her palace they might be. Every home and building throughout the Land of Oz was to be decorated with banners and bunting, and there were to be games, and plays, and a general good time for every one.

It was Ozma's custom on her birthday to give a grand feast at the palace, to which all her closest friends were invited. It was a queerly assorted company, indeed, for there are more quaint and unusual characters in Oz than in all the rest of the world, and Ozma was more interested in unusual people than in ordinary ones — just as you and I are.

On this especial birthday of the lovely girl Ruler, a long table was set in the royal Banquet Hall of the palace, at which were place-cards for the invited guests, and at one end of the great room was a smaller table, not so high, for Ozma's animal friends, whom she never forgot, and at the other end was a big table where all of the birthday gifts were to be arranged.

When the guests arrived, they placed their gifts on this table and then found their places at the banquet table. And, after the guests were all placed, the animals entered in a solemn procession and were placed at their table by Jellia Jamb. Then, while an orchestra hidden by a bank of roses and ferns played a march

The Magic of Oz

composed for the occasion, the Royal Ozma entered the Banquet Hall, attended by her Maids of Honor, and took her seat at the head of the table.

She was greeted by a cheer from all the assembled company, the animals adding their roars and growls and barks and mewing and cackling to swell the glad tumult, and then all seated themselves at their tables.

At Ozma's right sat the famous Scarecrow of Oz, whose straw-stuffed body was not beautiful, but whose happy nature and shrewd wit had made him a general favorite. On the left of the Ruler was placed the Tin Woodman, whose metal body had been brightly polished for this event. The Tin Woodman was the Emperor of the Winkie Country and one of the most important persons in Oz.

Next to the Scarecrow, Dorothy was seated, and next to her was Tik-Tok, the Clockwork Man, who had been wound up as tightly as his clockwork would permit, so he wouldn't interrupt the festivities by running down. Then came Aunt Em and Uncle Henry, Dorothy's own relations, two kindly old people who had a cozy home in the Emerald City and were very happy and contented there. Then Betsy Bobbin was seated, and next to her the droll and delightful Shaggy Man, who was a favorite wherever he went.

Chapter Twenty-Two

On the other side of the table, opposite the Tin Woodman was placed Trot, and next to her, Cap'n Bill. Then was seated Button Bright and Ojo the Lucky, and Dr. Pipt and his good wife Margalot, and the astonishing Frogman, who had come from the Yip country to be present at Ozma's birthday feast.

At the foot of the table, facing Ozma, was seated the queenly Glinda, the good Sorceress of Oz, for this was really the place of honor next to the head of the table where Ozma herself sat. On Glinda's right was the Little Wizard of Oz, who owed to Glinda all of the magical arts he knew. Then came Jinjur, a pretty girl farmer of whom Ozma and Dorothy were quite fond. The adjoining seat was occupied by the Tin Soldier, and next to him was Professor H. M. Wogglebug, T.E., of the Royal Athletic College.

On Glinda's left was placed the jolly Patchwork Girl, who was a little afraid of the Sorceress and so was likely to behave herself pretty well. The Shaggy Man's brother was beside the Patchwork Girl, and then came that interesting personage, Jack Pumpkinhead, who had grown a splendid big pumpkin for a new head to be worn on Ozma's birthday, and had carved a face on it that was even jollier in expression than the one he had last worn. New heads were not

The Magic of Oz

unusual with Jack, for the pumpkins did not keep long, and when the seeds — which served him as brains — began to get soft and mushy, he realized his head would soon spoil, and so he procured a new one from his great field of pumpkins — grown by him so that he need never lack a head.

You will have noticed that the company at Ozma's banquet table was somewhat mixed, but every one invited was a tried and trusted friend of the girl Ruler, and their presence made her quite happy.

No sooner had Ozma seated herself, with her back to the birthday table, than she noticed that all present were eyeing with curiosity and pleasure something behind her, for the gorgeous Magic Flower was blooming gloriously and the mammoth blossoms that quickly succeeded one another on the plant were beautiful to view and filled the entire room with their delicate fragrance. Ozma wanted to look, too, to see what all were staring at, but she controlled her curiosity because it was not proper that she should yet view her birthday gifts.

So the sweet and lovely Ruler devoted herself to her guests, several of whom, as the Sorcerer, the Tin Woodman, the Patchwork Girl, Tik-Tok, Jack Pumpkinhead and the Tin Soldier, never ate anything but

Chapter Twenty-Two

sat very politely in their places and tried to entertain those of the guests who did eat.

And, at the animal table, there was another interesting group, consisting of the Cowardly Lion, the Hungry Tiger, Toto—Dorothy's little shaggy black dog —Hank the Mule, the Pink Kitten, the Wooden Sawhorse, the Yellow Hen, and the Glass Cat. All of these had good appetites except the Sawhorse and the Glass Cat, and each was given a plentiful supply of the food it liked best.

Finally, when the banquet was nearly over and the ice-cream was to be served, four servants entered bearing a huge cake, all frosted and decorated with candy flowers. Around the edge of the cake was a row of lighted candles, and in the center were raised candy letters that spelled the words:

OZMA'S
Birthday Cake
from
Dorothy and the Wizard

" Oh, how beautiful! " cried Ozma, greatly delighted, and Dorothy said eagerly: " Now you must cut the cake, Ozma, and each of us will eat a piece with our ice-cream."

The Magic of Oz

Jellia Jamb brought a large golden knife with a jeweled handle, and Ozma stood up in her place and attempted to cut the cake. But as soon as the frosting in the center broke under the pressure of the knife there leaped from the cake a tiny monkey three inches high, and he was followed by another and another, until twelve monkeys stood on the tablecloth and bowed low to Ozma.

"Congratulations to our gracious Ruler!" they exclaimed in a chorus, and then they began a dance, so droll and amusing that all the company roared with laughter and even Ozma joined in the merriment. But after the dance the monkeys performed some wonderful acrobatic feats, and then they ran to the hollow of the cake and took out some band instruments of burnished gold—cornets, horns, drums, and the like—and forming into a procession the monkeys marched up and down the table playing a jolly tune with the ease of skilled musicians.

Dorothy was delighted with the success of her "Surprise Cake," and after the monkeys had finished their performance, the banquet came to an end.

Now was the time for Ozma to see her other presents, so Glinda the Good rose and, taking the girl Ruler by her hand, led her to the table where all her

The Magic of Oz

gifts were placed in magnificent array. The Magic Flower of course attracted her attention first, and Trot had to tell her the whole story of their adventures in getting it. The little girl did not forget to give due credit to the Glass Cat and the little Wizard, but it was really Cap'n Bill who bravely carried the golden flowerpot away from the enchanted Isle.

Ozma thanked them all, and said she would place the Magic Flower in her boudoir where she might enjoy its beauty and fragrance continually. But now she discovered the marvelous gown woven by Glinda and her maidens from strands drawn from pure emeralds, and being a girl who loved pretty clothes, Ozma's ecstasy at being presented with this exquisite gown may well be imagined. She could hardly wait to put it on, but the table was loaded with other pretty gifts and the night was far spent before the happy girl Ruler had examined all her presents and thanked those who had lovingly donated them.

The Fountain of Oblivion

CHAPTER 23

The morning after the birthday fete, as the Wizard and
Dorothy were walking in the
grounds of the palace, Ozma
came out and joined them,
saying:

"I want to hear more of
your adventures in the Forest
of Gugu, and how you were
able to get those dear little
monkeys to use in Dorothy's
Surprise Cake."

So they sat down on a mar-

255

ble bench near to the fountain of the Water of Oblivion, and between them Dorothy and the Wizard related their adventures.

"I was dreadfully fussy while I was a woolly lamb," said Dorothy, "for it didn't feel good, a bit. And I wasn't quite sure, you know, that I'd ever get to be a girl again."

"You might have been a woolly lamb yet, if I hadn't happened to have discovered that Magic Transformation Word," declared the Wizard.

"But what became of the walnut and the hickory-nut into which you transformed those dreadful beast magicians?" inquired Ozma.

"Why, I'd almost forgotten them," was the reply; "but I believe they are still here in my pocket."

Then he searched in his pockets and brought out the two nuts and showed them to her.

Ozma regarded them thoughtfully.

"It isn't right to leave any living creatures in such helpless forms," said she. "I think, Wizard, you ought to transform them into their natural shapes again."

"But I don't know what their natural shapes are," he objected, "for of course the forms of mixed animals which they had assumed were not natural to them. And you must not forget, Ozma, that their natures were cruel and mischievous, so if I bring them back to life they might cause us a great deal of trouble."

"Nevertheless," said the Ruler of Oz, "we must free them from their present enchantments. When you restore them to their natural forms we will discover who they really are, and surely we need not fear any two people, even though they prove to be magicians and our enemies."

"I am not so sure of that," protested the Wizard, with a shake of his bald head. "The one bit of magic I robbed them of — which was the word of transformation — is so simple, yet so powerful, that neither Glinda nor I can equal it. It isn't all in the word, you know, it's the way the word is pronounced. So if the two strange magicians have other magic of the same sort, they might prove very dangerous to us, if we liberated them."

"I've an idea!" exclaimed Dorothy. "I'm no wizard, and no fairy, but if you do as I say, we needn't fear these people at all."

"What is your thought, my dear?" asked Ozma.

"Well," replied the girl, "here is this fountain of the Water of Oblivion, and that's what put the notion

The Magic of Oz

into my head. When the Wizard speaks that ter'ble word that will change 'em back to their real forms, he can make 'em dreadful thirsty, too, and we'll put a cup right here by the fountain, so it'll be handy. Then they'll drink the water and forget all the magic they ever knew — and everything else, too."

"That's not a bad idea," said the Wizard, looking at Dorothy approvingly.

"It's a very *good* idea," declared Ozma. "Run for a cup, Dorothy."

So Dorothy ran to get a cup, and while she was gone the Wizard said:

"I don't know whether the real forms of these magicians are those of men or beasts. If they're beasts, they would not drink from a cup but might attack us at once and drink afterward. So it might be safer for us to have the Cowardly Lion and the Hungry Tiger here to protect us if necessary."

Ozma drew out a silver whistle which was attached to a slender gold chain and blew upon the whistle two shrill blasts. The sound, though not harsh, was very penetrating, and as soon as it reached the ears of the Cowardly Lion and the Hungry Tiger, the two huge beasts quickly came bounding toward them. Ozma explained to them what the Wizard was about to do, and told them to keep quiet unless danger threatened. So the two powerful guardians of the Ruler of Oz crouched beside the fountain and waited.

Dorothy returned and set the cup on the edge of the fountain. Then the Wizard placed the hickory-

nut beside the fountain and said in a solemn voice:

"I want you to resume your natural form, and to be very thirsty — **Pyrzqxgl!**"

In an instant there appeared, in the place of the hickory-nut, the form of Kiki Aru, the Hyup boy. He seemed bewildered, at first, as if trying to remember what had happened to him and why he was in this strange place. But he was facing the fountain, and the bubbling water reminded him that he was thirsty. Without noticing Ozma, the Wizard and Dorothy, who were behind him, he picked up the cup, filled it with the Water of Oblivion, and drank it to the last drop.

He was now no longer thirsty, but he felt more bewildered than ever, for now he could remember nothing at all — not even his name or where he came from. He looked around the beautiful garden with a pleased expression, and then, turning, he beheld Ozma and the Wizard and Dorothy regarding him curiously and the two great beasts crouching behind them.

Kiki Aru did not know who they were, but he thought Ozma very lovely and Dorothy very pleasant. So he smiled at them — the same innocent, happy smile that a baby might have indulged in, and that pleased Dorothy, who seized his hand and led him to a seat beside her on the bench.

" Why, I thought you were a dreadful magician," she exclaimed, " and you're only a boy! "

" What is a magician? " he asked, " and what is a boy? "

" Don't you know? " inquired the girl.

Chapter Twenty-Three

Kiki shook his head. Then he laughed.

"I do not seem to know anything," he replied.

"It's very curious," remarked the Wizard. "He wears the dress of the Munchkins, so he must have

lived at one time in the Munchkin Country. Of course the boy can tell us nothing of his history or his family, for he has forgotten all that he ever knew."

"He seems a nice boy, now that all the wickedness

The Magic of Oz

has gone from him," said Ozma. "So we will keep him here with us and teach him our ways — to be true and considerate of others."

"Why, in that case, it's lucky for him he drank the Water of Oblivion," said Dorothy.

"It is indeed," agreed the Wizard. "But the remarkable thing, to me, is how such a young boy ever learned the secret of the Magic Word of Transformation. Perhaps his companion, who is at present this walnut, was the real magician, although I seem to remember that it was this boy in the beast's form who whispered the Magic Word into the hollow tree, where I overheard it."

"Well, we will soon know who the other is," suggested Ozma. "He may prove to be another Munchkin boy."

The Wizard placed the walnut near the fountain and said, as slowly and solemnly as before:

"I want you to resume your natural form, and to be very thirsty — **P y r z q x g l !**"

Then the walnut disappeared and Ruggedo the Nome stood in its place. He also was facing the fountain, and he reached for the cup, filled it, and was about to drink when Dorothy exclaimed:

"Why, it's the old Nome King!"

Ruggedo swung around and faced them, the cup still in his hand.

"Yes," he said in an angry voice, "it's the old Nome King, and I'm going to conquer all Oz and be re-

venged on you for kicking me out of my throne." He looked around a moment, and then continued: "There isn't an egg in sight, and I'm stronger than all of you people put together! I don't know how I came here, but I'm going to fight the fight of my life — and I'll win!"

His long white hair and beard waved in the breeze; his eyes flashed hate and vengeance, and so astonished and shocked were they by the sudden appearance of this old enemy of the Oz people that they could only stare at him in silence and shrink away from his wild glare.

Ruggedo laughed. He drank the water, threw the cup on the ground and said fiercely:

" And now — and now — and — "

His voice grew gentle. He rubbed his forehead with a puzzled air and stroked his long beard.

"What was I going to say?" he asked, pleadingly.

"Don't you remember?" said the Wizard.

" No; I've forgotten."

" Who *are* you?" asked Dorothy.

He tried to think. " I — I'm sure I don't know," he stammered.

"Don't you know who *we* are, either?" questioned the girl.

"I haven't the slightest idea," said the Nome.

"Tell us who this Munchkin boy is," suggested Ozma.

Ruggedo looked at the boy and shook his head.

"He's a stranger to me. You are all strangers. I — I'm a stranger to myself," he said.

Then he patted the Lion's head and murmured, "Good doggie!" and the Lion growled indignantly.

"What shall we do with him?" asked the Wizard, perplexed.

"Once before the wicked old Nome came here to conquer us, and then, as now, he drank of the Water of Oblivion and became harmless. But we sent him back to the Nome Kingdom, where he soon learned the old evil ways again."

The Magic of Oz

" For that reason," said Ozma, we must find a place for him in the Land of Oz, and keep him here. For here he can learn no evil and will always be as innocent of guile as our own people."

And so the wandering ex-King of the Nomes found a new home, a peaceful and happy home, where he was quite content and passed his days in innocent enjoyment.

1

THE OZ SERIES BY L. FRANK BAUM

Published by
For Your Knowledge

available from the Ann Arbor Media Group
at Amazon.com and your local retailer

Which ones do you have?